Mankind: A Medieval Morality Play (A Retelling)

David Bruce

Published by David Bruce, 2023.

This is a work of fiction. Similarities to real people, places, or events are entirely coincidental.

MANKIND: A MEDIEVAL MORALITY PLAY (A RETELLING)

First edition. January 20, 2023.

ISBN: 979-8201200305

Written by David Bruce.

Table of Contents

Dedication

Dedicated to Carl Eugene Bruce and Josephine Saturday Bruce

My father, Carl Eugene Bruce, died on 24 October 2013. He used to work for Ohio Power, and at one time, his job was to shut off the electricity of people who had not paid their bills. He sometimes would find a home with an impoverished mother and some children. Instead of shutting off their electricity, he would tell the mother that she needed to pay her bill or soon her electricity would be shut off. He would write on a form that no one was home when he stopped by because if no one was home he did not have to shut off their electricity.

The best good deed that anyone ever did for my father occurred after a storm that knocked down many power lines. He and other linemen worked long hours and got wet and cold. Their feet were freezing because water got into their boots and soaked their socks. Fortunately, a kind woman gave my father and the other linemen dry socks to wear.

My mother, Josephine Saturday Bruce, died on 14 June 2003. She used to work at a store that sold clothing. One day, an impoverished mother with a baby clothed in rags walked into the store and started shoplifting in an interesting way: The mother took the rags off her baby and dressed the infant in new clothing. My mother knew that this mother could not afford to buy the clothing, but she helped the mother dress her baby and then she watched as the mother walked out of the store without paying.

***

The doing of good deeds is important. As a free person, you can choose to live your life as a good person or as a bad person. To be a good person, do good deeds. To be a bad person, do bad deeds. If you do good deeds, you will become good. If you do bad deeds, you will become bad. To become the person you want to be, act as if you already are that kind of person. Each of us chooses what kind of person we will become. To become a good person, do the things a good person does. To become a bad person, do the things a bad person does. The opportunity to take action to become the kind of person you want to be is yours.

Human beings have free will. According to the Babylonian Niddah 16b, whenever a baby is to be conceived, the Lailah (angel in charge of contraception) takes the drop of semen that will result in the conception and asks God, "Sovereign of the Universe, what is going to be the fate of this drop? Will it develop into a robust or into a weak person? An intelligent or a stupid person? A wealthy or a poor person?" The Lailah asks all these questions, but it does not ask, "Will it develop into a righteous or a wicked person?" The answer to that question lies in the decisions to be freely made by the human being that is the result of the conception.

A Buddhist monk visiting a class wrote this on the chalkboard: "EVERYONE WANTS TO SAVE THE WORLD, BUT NO ONE WANTS TO HELP MOM DO THE DISHES." The students laughed, but the monk then said, "Statistically, it's highly unlikely that any of you will ever have the opportunity to run into a burning orphanage and rescue an infant. But, in the smallest gesture of kindness — a warm smile, holding the door for the person behind you, shoveling the driveway of the elderly person next door — you have committed an act of immeasurable profundity, because to each of us, our life is our universe."

Educate Yourself
Read Like A Wolf Eats
Be Excellent to Each Other
Books Then, Books Now, Books Forever

***

In this retelling, as in all my retellings, I have tried to make the work of literature accessible to modern readers who may lack some of the knowledge about mythology, religion, and history that the literary work's contemporary audience had.

Do you know a language other than English? If you do, I give you permission to translate this book, copyright your translation, publish or self-publish it, and keep all the royalties for yourself. (Do give me credit, of course, for the original retelling.)

I would like to see my retellings of classic literature used in schools, so I give permission to the country of Finland (and all other countries) to give copies of any or all of my retellings to all students forever. I also give permission to the state of Texas (and all other states) to give copies of any or all of my retellings to all students forever. I also give permission to all teachers to give copies of any or all of my retellings to all students forever. Of course, libraries are welcome to use my eBooks for free.

Teachers need not actually teach my retellings. Teachers are welcome to give students copies of my eBooks as background material. For example, if they are teaching Homer's *Iliad* and *Odyssey*, teachers are welcome to give students copies of my *Virgil's* Aeneid: *A Retelling in Prose* and tell students, "Here's another ancient epic you may want to read in your spare time."

CAST OF CHARACTERS

MISCHIEF: Evil

NEW GUISE: the World (New Fashion, Latest Fashion, New Look, New Mode of Behavior)

NOWADAYS: the World (Living for Today, Up-To-Dateness)

NOUGHT: the World (Nothingness, Worthlessness, Pointlessness)

MANKIND: Soul and Body

TITIVILLUS: Satan (All Vile Things)

NOTES:

In the Middle Ages, "mischief" had a much stronger meaning of evil than it does today. Today, "mischief" can be an annoying prank. Then, "mischief" could be an attempt to send your soul to Hell forever.

Mischief is hierarchically above these three demons: New Guise, Nowadays, and Nought.

Titivillus is the main opponent to human salvation. He is hierarchically above Mischief.

These demons have knowledge of saints. No demon is an atheist. Demons don't believe in God: Demons *know* that God exists. These demons also have a good knowledge of scripture and of the saints.

The three main opponents to human salvation are the World, the Body, and the Devil.

The World is the fallen World. It is the World after the fall of Humankind in the Garden of Eden.

All human beings sin, but if a sinner sincerely repents sin, God will be merciful.

Mercy in this play may be played in the clothing of a Catholic priest.

This book calls New Guise, Nowadays, and Nought demons, but they could be unrepentant human sinners.

The Middle Ages occurred before the Protestant Reformation, so all Christians are Catholic or Eastern Orthodox.

In this society, a person of higher rank would use "thou," "thee," "thine," and "thy" when referring to a person of lower rank. (These terms were also used affectionately and between equals.) A person of lower rank would use "you" and "your" when referring to a person of higher rank.

The word "corn" means "grain": oats, rye, wheat, etc. Maize had not yet been imported from North America when this play was written. *Mankind* was written c. 1470. Columbus brought maize to Spain in 1493.

Mankind is Humankind.

***

EDITIONS:

Bevington, David. *Medieval Drama*. Atlanta, etc.: Houghton Mifflin Company. 1975. Includes *Mankind*.

A Critical Edition of the Medieval Play Mankind. Editors: Frank Knittel and Grosvenor Fattic. Lewiston, NY; Queenston, Canada; Lampeter, UK: The Edwin Mellon Press, 1995.

Mankind. Edited by Kathleen M. Ashley and Gerard NeCastro. Kalamazoo, MI: Medieval Institute Publications, 2010.

https://d.lib.rochester.edu/teams/text/ashley-and-necastro-mankind

Mankind: An Acting Edition. Edited by Peter Meredith. Leeds: Alumnus, 1997.

Here is an online modern-spelling edition:

https://bidoonism.files.wordpress.com/2019/12/jhk___mankind_archive.pdf

https://d.lib.rochester.edu/teams/text/ashley-and-necastro-mankind

Here is another online modern-spelling edition:

https://web.archive.org/web/20160724104710/
http://research.uvu.edu/mcdonald/3610/mankind.html

Here is an online adaptation of *Mankind* by Lauren Nypaver, Brandi King, and Stacy Weaver of Winthrop University in Rock Hill, South Carolina.

http://faculty.winthrop.edu/kosterj/engl325/mankind2000.htm

CRITICISM:

Coogan, Sister Mary Phillippa. *An Interpretation of the Moral Play, Mankind: A Dissertation.* Washington DC: The Catholic University of America Press, 1947.

YOUTUBE:

Here is a YouTube performance of *Mankind* that is directed and translated by Makoto Takata:

https://www.youtube.com/watch?v=0j-J9QXrt3A

ONLINE MIDDLE ENGLISH DICTIONARIES:

Middle English Dictionary — University of Michigan

https://quod.lib.umich.edu/m/middle-english-dictionary/
dictionary

Middle English Dictionary — LEXILOGOS (Includes useful links)

https://www.lexilogos.com/english/english_middle.htm

CHAPTER 1

— Scene 1 —

— Education —

Mercy said:

"The very founder and beginner of our first creation is God. Among us sinful wretches, God ought to be magnified and praised because in response to our disobedience he showed no anger but sent His own Son to us to be torn and crucified. Our dutiful service to Him should be offered. Although God was Lord of all and made all things out of nothing, in order to have the sinful sinner revived, and for the sinful sinner's redemption, God sacrificed His own son.

"It may be said and verified that Humankind was dearly bought and was redeemed at a very high price. By the piteous death of Jesus, Humankind had his remedy and rescue from sin. By Christ's glorious passion, that blessed act of cleaning, Humankind was purged of their sin that they wretchedly had wrought."

John 3:16 states, "*For God so loved the world, that he gave his only begotten Son, that whosoever believeth in him should not perish, but have everlasting life*" (King James Version).

Mercy continued:

"O worthy audience members, I beseech you to rectify your manner of life and with humility and reverence to have a return to this blessed Prince Who does glorify our nature so that you may share in His reward, which is salvation.

"I have been the true means for your restoration. Mercy is my name, and I mourn for your offence and sin. Don't divert yourselves from the true path in times of temptation, so that you may be acceptable to God at your going from here to the afterlife. The great mercy of God, which is of most pre-eminence, by the intercession of

Our Lady — the Virgin Mary — is ever abundant and bountiful for the sinful creature who will repent his negligence and sinfulness. I pray to God that at your times of most need mercy will be your advocate and will protect you."

Psalm 25:10 states, "*All the paths of the LORD are mercy and truth unto such as keep his covenant and testimonies*" (King James Version).

Mercy continued:

"In good works I advise you, sovereigns, to be persevering to purify your souls, so that they are not corrupt, for your spiritual enemy will make his boast if he may interrupt and disrupt your good conditions and virtuous life.

"O you sovereigns here who sit and you brethren here who stand right up, don't pin your happiness in things transitory. Don't look at the earth but instead lift up your eyes. See how the limbs daily worship the Head. Who the Head is truly I shall instruct you: I mean our Savior, Who was compared to a lamb, and His saints are the limbs who daily He does satisfy with the precious river of life-giving blood that runs from his side."

John 19:34 states, "*But one of the soldiers with a spear pierced his side, and forthwith came there out blood and water*" (King James Version).

Mercy continued:

"There is no such food, by water or by land or anywhere, that is so precious, so glorious, so needful for our purpose, for it has freed Humankind from the bitter bond of the mortal and deadly enemy, that venomous serpent, from which may God preserve and protect you all at the Last Judgment! For certainly there shall be a strict examination: The corn [grain] shall be saved, but the chaff shall be burnt. I beseech you heartily, have this forethought and consider it closely."

Matthew 3:12 states, "*Whose fan is in his hand, and he will th[o]roughly purge his floor, and gather his wheat into the garner; but he will burn up the chaff with unquenchable fire*" (King James Version).

Luke 3:17 states, "*Whose fan is in his hand, and he will th[o]roughly purge his floor, and will gather the wheat into his garner; but the chaff he will burn with fire unquenchable*" (King James Version).

Mischief entered the scene and said:

"I beseech you heartily, leave your threshing. Leave your chaff, leave your corn, leave your chatter. Your intelligence is little, your head is big, and you are full of preaching.

"But, sir, I ask you this question to explain:

"Mishmash, driff-draff,

"Some was corn and some was chaff,

"My mother said my name was Raff [Ralph]."

Mischief continued:

"Unshut your lock — that is, open your purse — and take out a halfpenny."

"Unshut your lock and take out a halfpenny" also means "open your mouth and speak something worthwhile."

The metaphorical halfpenny would be the knowledge that would be gained if Mercy could explain the "question," which is not explicit.

The question may be this: Where does Mischief [Raff] fit? Is he among the corn or is he among the chaff?

"Mishmash" is a confused jumble.

"Driff-draff" is "riff-raff," aka "disreputable people."

"Raff" means "disreputable people."

"Riff" is a variant of "rife" and means "widespread" or "prevalent."

The answer could be that Mischief fits with the chaff, but that if Mischief sincerely repents his sin, then he would fit with the corn.

Mischief is a demon, which is a fallen angel. In order to sin, a being must have free will. Mischief used his free will to choose to do evil.

Can demons use their free will to choose to do good? Probably not. Beings, including human beings, can lose their free will. A human being who chooses over and over to do evil can become a slave to their desire to do evil and can become incapable of making the effort of will to choose to do good.

According to Dante's *Inferno*, the sinners in the Inferno are no longer capable of repenting. They will stay in the Inferno forever. Lucifer is one sinner who is being punished in the Inferno forever. The allegorical figure Mischief [Evil] is unlikely to be able to repent, and so yes, he is Raff and he is chaff.

Who is Mischief's mother? God created the angels.

The Bible includes maternal images of God:

Isaiah 42:14 states, "*I have long time holden my peace; I have been still, and refrained myself: now will I cry like a travailing woman; I will destroy and devour at once*" (King James Version).

Isaiah 66:13 states, "*As one whom his mother comforteth, so will I comfort you; and ye shall be comforted in Jerusalem*" (King James Version).

Some Christians regard Mary as the mother of God because she is the mother of Jesus, Who is one part of the Trinity.

Mercy said, "Why have you come here, brother? You were not wanted here."

Why is Mischief here?

Mischief answered:

"Sir, for a winter corn-thresher, I have hired."

This is ambiguous. It could mean: 1) I have hired someone to work as a winter corn-thresher, or 2) I have hired myself out — been employed — as a winter corn-thresher.

Mischief is unlikely to literally do either, as he is unlikely to work or to do good things. (Growing and harvesting food is one of the most important activities of human beings.) In addition, threshing is not done in the winter; it is done in between harvesting and winnowing. Also, as we shall soon learn, the present time in the play is the time for sowing seeds.

Spring wheat is harvested in the summer and autumn. Winter wheat is harvested in the spring and summer. Once the grain has dried, it is threshed. (With modern machinery — i.e., combine harvesters — harvesting and threshing occur at the same time.)

Threshing can be done in the winter, but threshing earlier can reduce the loss of grain. If not threshed, the grain can accumulate moisture, which can lead to the growth of mold.

But is Mischief figuratively a corn thresher? Yes. He will try to get Mankind to turn to evil: to figuratively go from being corn to being chaff and straw.

Chaff is the dried husks of grain; straw is the dried stalks. Both can be used for animal fodder, and both can be burned.

Mischief continued:

"And you said the corn should be saved and the chaff should be burnt, but the author of the following verse proves that is wrong:

"*Corn servit bredibus, chaff horsibus, straw firibusque.*"

This mock-Latin means: Corn serves to make bread, chaff serves to feed horses, and straw serves to feed the fire.

Mischief continued:

"This is as much as to say, to your ignorant understanding, that the corn shall serve to make bread at the next baking.

"*Chaff horsibus et reliqua.*"

This mock-Latin means: Chaff serves to feed horses, and the rest."

Mischief continued:

"The chaff shall be good provender for horses, and when a man is very cold, the straw may be burned, and so forth, et cetera."

Is Chaff making a comic "defense" for being a demon? Demons are the equivalent of chaff and straw, while saved human beings are the equivalent of corn.

Chaff and straw have purposes.

Chaff can feed horses, but not human beings, for chaff is indigestible to human beings.

And straw can be burned to warm human beings — such as the sinners in Hell.

"Leave us, good brother!" Mercy said. "You are at fault to interrupt thus my sweet, pleasant talking."

"Sir, I have neither horse not saddle," Mischief said, "and therefore I may not ride."

"Then get you forth on foot, brother, in God's name!" Mercy said.

Mischief said:

"I say, sir, I have come here to make you sport."

"To make you sport" is ambiguous: 1) to entertain you, or 2) to make fun of you.

Mischief continued:

"Yet you did not order me to go out *in the devil's name*, and so I will stay."

[A leaf is missing from the manuscript here. Apparently, Mischief continued to torment Mercy, and then Mischief left. New Guise, Nowadays, and Nought then entered the scene and engaged in horseplay.]

New Guise and Nowadays were hitting Nought to make him dance.

When not tormenting Humankind, these demons bullied each other.

New Guise said, "And ho! Minstrels, play the common dance tune. Lay on with your sticks until his belly burst!"

"Belly" can mean 1) drum-skin, or 2) Nought's stomach.

The sticks may be the arms and hands of New Guise and Nowadays. They may be beating out dance percussion on Nought's belly.

"Suppose I break my neck," Nought said. "What then?"

"I don't care, by Saint Anne!" New Guise said.

Saint Anne is the patron saint of the infertile. She is also the mother of Mary, and therefore she is the grandmother of Jesus.

"Leap about lively!" Nowadays said. "Thou are a lively man. Let us be merry while we are here!"

"Shall I break my neck to entertain you?" Nought complained.

"Therefore, be careful about what you say," Nowadays said.

If Nought says the wrong thing, the other demons might break his neck.

"I curse you all!" Nought said. "Here is an accursed company. Have at it then with a merry cheer!"

New Guise, Nowadays, and Nought danced.

"Stop," Mercy said. "Stop this revelry, sirs! Stop!"

"Stop, good Adam?" Nowadays said. "Stop? This is no part of thy play. It is no concern of yours."

A "good Adam" is a "good old man."

Nought said:

"Yes, by the Virgin Mary, I ask you to stop, for I don't love this reveling."

Nought then said to Mercy:

"Come forth, good father, I ask you! With a little effort, you may try. At once, off with your clothes — your priest's vestments — if you will play. Go to it! For I have had a pretty little share of dancing."

Nought had had enough dancing, so now he wanted Mercy to dance.

"Nay, brother," Mercy said. "I will not dance."

"If you will, sir, my brother Nowadays will make you prance," New Guise said.

"With all my heart, sir, if I may assist you," Nowadays said. "You may try dancing with a little step."

Nought said to Mercy:

"You, sir, will you do well?

"Don't dance with them, I advise you, for I have danced somewhat too violently. I tell you that it is a narrow space: There's not much room.

"But, sir, I believe I heard you speak about us three."

The priest — Mercy — had spoken about New Guise, Nowadays, and Nought, perhaps in the pages missing from the manuscript. That had had the effect of summoning them away from their sleeping and eating.

Sloth and gluttony are two of the seven deadly sins. The others are lust, gluttony, pride, greed, and envy.

"Christ's curse had you, therefore, for I was asleep," New Guise said.

"And I had the cup in my hand, ready to go to dinner," Nowadays said. "Therefore, sir, curtly, we greet you well."

"Few words, few and well placed!" Mercy said.

He was sarcastic in his "praise."

The demons had greeted Mercy curtly; if they had greeted him courteously, they would have greeted him well.

New Guise said, "Sir, it is the new guise and the new fashion: many words and curtly offered. This is the new guise, every bit."

Mercy prayed, "Our Lady, help! How these wretches delight in their sinful ways!"

"Our Lady" is the Virgin Mary.

Nowadays said, "Say nothing against the new guise nowadays! Thou shall find us tough fighters at all trials. Beware! You may soon lick — taste — a buffet."

A "buffet" is a blow.

"He was well occupied who brought you, brethren," Mercy said.

Who brought the demons? Mischief, perhaps. But Mercy, by speaking about the demons (in the lines on the missing sheet of paper?) may have inadvertently "summoned" the demons.

Nought said:

"I heard you call 'New Guise, Nowadays, Nought' — all these three together. If you say that I lie, I shall make you slither and crawl on the ground.

"Lo, I take you here a trip!"

He tripped Mercy.

"Tell me your names," Mercy said. "I don't know you."

If Mercy did not know the demons' names, he could not have summoned them by name. He could, however, have criticized the kinds of behavior these demons demonstrate.

"New Guise, I am," New Guise said.

Nowadays said, "I am Nowadays."

"Nought said, "I am Nought."

"By Jesus Christ, Who dearly redeemed me, you betray many men," Mercy said.

New Guise said:

"Betray! Nay, nay, sir, nay! We make them both fresh and gay — cheerful and carefree.

"But what is your name, sir? I ask you so that we may know you."

"Mercy is my name by denomination," Mercy said. "I conceive you have but a little favor in my communication."

New Guise said:

"Aye, aye! Your body is full of English Latin."

Mercy was using Latinate words such as "denomination" and "communication." *Nomen* is Latin for "name." The Latin *communicare* means "to share." English takes many words from many languages.

As a priest, Mercy was well educated and knew Latin and so he was able to use big words.

New Guise continued:

"I am afraid your body will burst.

"*Pravo te*, said the butcher to me when I stole a leg of mutton."

Pravo te is Latin for "I curse you."

New Guise continued:

"You are a very learned scholar."

Nowadays said:

"I ask you heartily, worshipful clerk, to have this English translated into Latin:

"*I have eaten a dishful of curds,*

"And I have shitten your mouth full of turds.

Mercy did not say this to Nowadays.

"Now open your satchel — your mouth — with Latin words and say that to me in a learned manner!"

The Latin translation is this:

Edi catino butyrum,

Et foedat os tuum plenum excrementum.

"Also, I have a wife; her name is Rachel. Between her and me was a great battle, and gladly from you I would hear you tell who was the most master."

"Thy wife Rachel was the most master," Nought said. "I dare bet twenty lice."

Nowadays and his wife, Rachel, do not have a love relationship.

In the Bible, a different Rachel is the wife of Jacob, and she is the mother of Joseph and Benjamin. The relationship of Rachel and Jacob was one of love. Jacob was tricked into marrying Leah, Rachel's older sister. He loved Rachel, and he worked seven more years for Rachel's father so that he could marry her, too.

Genesis 29:18-35 (King James Version) states:

18 And Jacob loved Rachel; and said, I will serve thee seven years for Rachel thy younger daughter.

19 And Laban said, It is better that I give her to thee, than that I should give her to another man: abide with me.

20 And Jacob served seven years for Rachel; and they seemed unto him but a few days, for the love he had to her.

21 And Jacob said unto Laban, Give me my wife, for my days are fulfilled, that I may go in unto her.

22 And Laban gathered together all the men of the place, and made a feast.

23 And it came to pass in the evening, that he took Leah his daughter, and brought her to him; and he went in unto her.

24 And Laban gave unto his daughter Leah Zilpah his maid for an handmaid.

25 And it came to pass, that in the morning, behold, it was Leah: and he said to Laban, What is this thou hast done unto me? did not I serve with thee for Rachel? wherefore then hast thou beguiled me?

26 And Laban said, It must not be so done in our country, to give the younger before the firstborn.

27 Fulfil her week, and we will give thee this also for the service which thou shalt serve with me yet seven other years.

28 And Jacob did so, and fulfilled her week: and he gave him Rachel his daughter to wife also.

The marriage feast may have lasted seven days, and Laban, Leah's father, wanted Jacob to respect the marriage feast and Leah. In addition, the seven days was a honeymoon period.

Nowadays said, "Who spoke to thee, fool? Thou are not wise! Go and do that which pertains to thy duty: *Osculare fundamentum!*"

The Latin means: Kiss [my?] ass!

Nought said, "Lo, master, lo, here is a pardon belly-met: It is a satisfying — a belly-full — pardon. It is granted by Pope Pockett. If you will put your nose in his wife's socket, you shall have forty days of pardon."

A pardon remitted the punishment for sin. Often, pardons could be bought with money. Such a system led to abuse.

According to the *Oxford English Dictionary*, one meaning of nose is a "projecting part."

"His wife's socket" means "his wife's hole."

"This idle language you shall repent," Mercy said. "Out of this place, I wish you went."

New Guise said:

"We all three shall go away from here with one assent: We are all agreed to go. My spiritual father is displeased with our eloquence. Therefore, I will no longer tarry here.

"May God and blessed Mary bring you, master, to the number of the demonical friary!"

"The demonical friary" are clergy who are in Hell or will go to Hell.

Nowadays said:

"Come wind, come rain,

"Though I come never again!

"May the devil put out both your eyes!"

"Though I come never again!" means "Though I never come back again!"

Nowadays then said:

"Fellows, we go away from here quickly."

Nought said:

"We go away from here! We go the way of the devil! Here is the door; here is the way.

"Farewell, gentle Geoffrey. I pray God give you good night!"

New Guise, Nowadays, and Nought departed together, singing.

Mercy said:

"Thanked be God, we have a fair deliverance of these three unthrifty, wasteful guests: We are well rid of them. They know very little what is the place ordained for them.

"I can prove by reason that they are worse than beasts:

"A beast acts according to his natural instinct. You may conceive by their disport and behavior that their joy and delight is in derision and mockery of their own Christ to his dishonor.

"This condition of living, it is harmful.

"Beware, thereof, for it is worse than any felony or treason. How may it be excused before the Judge of all when for every idle word we must give a justification for and account for the way we have our life?"

Matthew 12.36-7 (King James Version) states:

36 But I say unto you, That every idle word that men shall speak, they shall give account thereof in the day of judgment.

37 For by thy words thou shalt be justified, and by thy words thou shalt be condemned.

Mercy continued:

"They have great ease and are very carefree; therefore, they will take no thought about the future. They are reckless. But what then when the angel of Heaven shall blow the trumpet on the Day of Judgment and say to the transgressors who wickedly have wrought sin, 'Come forth unto your Judge and yield your account of your life'?"

Matthew 12.36 states, "*But I say unto you, That every idle word that men shall speak, they shall give account thereof in the day of judgment*" (King James Version).

Mercy continued:

"Then shall I, Mercy, begin sorely and bitterly to weep. Neither comfort nor counsel and advice shall be had there. But such as they have sown, such shall they reap."

Galatians 6.7-8 (King James Version) states:

7 Be not deceived; God is not mocked: for whatsoever a man soweth, that shall he also reap.

8 For he that soweth to his flesh shall of the flesh reap corruption; but he that soweth to the Spirit shall of the Spirit reap life everlasting.

Mercy continued:

"They are wanton and joyful now, but then they shall be sad.

"The good new guise — mode of behavior — nowadays I will not forbid. I counsel against the vicious guise — the evil mode of behavior. I pray to have me excused. I need not to counsel against it, and I need not to speak of it. Your reason will tell you the proper mode of behavior.

"Take that which is to be taken and leave that which is to be refused."

1 Thessalonians 5.21 states, "*Prove [Test] all things; hold fast that which is good*" (King James Version).

Carrying a spade, Mankind entered the scene.

Mankind said:

"From the earth and from the clay, we have our propagation and birth. By the providence and foresight of God, we thus have our origin, to whose mercy I recommend this whole congregation: I hope unto His bliss you are all predestinated and destined for grace.

"Every man according to his place I trust shall participate and shall have his share if we will mortify our carnal, fleshly condition and our voluntary, willful desires that always are perverted. We must renounce them and place ourselves under God's provision and care.

"My name is Mankind. I have my composition of a body and of a soul, which by their nature are in conflict. Between them is a great division. He that should be subject, now has the victory."

In other words: the body should be subject to the soul, but now the body is victorious and is the master over the soul.

Mankind continued:

"This is to me a lamentable story: to see my flesh to have governance of my soul. Where the good-wife [wife] is the master, the good-man [husband] may be sorry. I may both sigh and sob; this is a piteous remembrance."

Ephesians 5:22-25 (King James Version) states:

22 Wives, submit yourselves unto your own husbands, as unto the Lord.

23 For the husband is the head of the wife, even as Christ is the head of the church: and he is the saviour of the body.

24 Therefore as the church is subject unto Christ, so let the wives be to their own husbands in every thing.

25 Husbands, love your wives, even as Christ also loved the church, and gave himself for it;

Mankind continued:

"O thou my soul, so subtle and pure in thy substance, alas, what was thy fortune and thy chance and thy fate to be joined with my flesh, that stinking dunghill?

"Our Lady, help! Sovereigns, it causes my soul much distress to see the flesh prosperous and the soul trodden under foot. I shall go to yonder man and appeal to him. I will make trial of him. I trust to ghostly — spiritual — solace that he will be my remedy."

Mankind went to Mercy, knelt, and said:

"All hail, worthy father! You are welcome to this house. You have participation in and access to the true wisdom. My body with my soul is always at war.

"I ask you, for holy charity, for your support.

"I ask you heartily for your spiritual comfort. I am unsteadfast in living; my name is Mankind. My spiritual enemy the devil will have a great delight in sinfully guiding me if he may see me end my life as a sinful man."

Mercy said to Mankind:

"May Christ send you good comfort! You are welcome, my friend. Stand up on your feet; I ask you to please rise."

Mankind stood up.

Mercy continued:

"My name is Mercy; you are to me very near and welcome. I will advise you to eschew vice."

Mankind said:

"O Mercy, you are the well and fountain and source of all grace and virtue. I have heard from very worshipful divines that you are next to God and near to his counsel. God has you in His confidence. He has set you above all his works.

"O, your lovely words to my soul are sweeter than honey."

Mercy said:

"The temptation of the flesh you must resist like a man, for there is always a battle between the soul and the body: *Vita hominis est milicia super terram.*"

The Latin means: The life of man on the earth is a battle (or a warfare).

Some translations of Job 7:1 state that Humankind's life upon the earth is a warfare.

Job 7:1 states, "*Is there not an appointed time to man upon earth? are not his days also like the days of a hireling?*" (King James Version).

Mercy continued:

"Attack your spiritual enemy and be Christ's own knight. Never be a coward against your adversary. If you will be crowned, you must necessarily fight. Mean well and God will be your ally.

"Remember, my friend, the time of continuance — your lifetime — on Earth. So help me, God, it is but a cherry time: a brief time. Spend it well; serve God with heart's loyalty and faith."

Cherry blossoms are beautiful, but they last only a short time.

Mercy continued:

"Don't distemper and sicken your brain with good ale nor with wine.

"Measure — that is, moderation — is treasure. I don't forbid you the use of alcohol. Measure yourself always, be moderate, and beware of excess.

"The superfluous guise I desire always that you refuse. When nature has enough, immediately cease.

"If a man has a horse and keeps him not too well-fed, he may then rule him at his own desire. If he — the horse — is fed too well, he will disobey and perhaps throw his master in the mire and mud."

Mercy was against the sin of gluttony, and he opposed also the overfeeding of horses. Of course, he was right to do so. Overfeeding a horse can result in giving the horse colic [intestinal and stomach problems], one symptom of which is lying down or rolling, which can result in the master's being in the mire and mud. An ill horse can be disinclined to obey its master.

New Guise, Nowadays, and Nought had been eavesdropping. Now New Guise spoke from a location where Mankind could not see him.

New Guise said:

"You say true, sir; you are no liar. I have fed my wife so well that she is my master. I have a great wound on my head, lo! And on it lies a plaster bandage, and another plaster bandage lies where I piss my peson."

A peson is literally a weighing instrument with a rod and balls. In the passage above, a peson is metaphorically a penis.

New Guise continued:

"If my wife were your horse, she would curse you all. You feed your horse in measure, so you are a 'wise' man. I think that if you were the king's palfreyman, aka stableman, then a good horse would be *geason*."

Geason means "scarce."

New Guise was criticizing Mercy's recommended feeding of horses. According to New Guise, overfeeding a wife results in a highly spirited wife. New Guise's overfed wife fights him. Mercy has said that an overfed horse will disobey the rider and may throw him in the mire and mud. New Guise is likely to consider that a spirited horse.

According to New Guise, not overfeeding a horse will result in horses without spirit and a good horse is a spirited horse, and so there will be few good horses. New Guise may even be saying that Mercy would starve horses.

Mercy, of course, would say that not overfeeding a horse will result in an obedient horse and an obedient horse is a good horse, and so there will be plentiful good horses.

Philosophers know that disputants need to define their terms. New Guise thinks that a good horse is a spirited horse; Mercy thinks that a good horse is an obedient horse.

In real life, of course, overfeeding horses is very bad. Overfeeding horses can cause colic, which can be fatal. Overfeeding a horse grain will result in a sick horse, not an spirited horse, as New Guise believes. New Guise's lack of knowledge about how to treat horses (and almost certainly his wife) well reflects his lack of knowledge about how to lead a good life.

New Guise is a bad reasoner, perhaps on purpose. When New Guise says that overfeeding results in a spirited horse (and a spirited wife), he is committing the fallacy of *non causa pro causa*, aka the False Cause fallacy. Overfeeding does not cause spiritedness; it causes illness.

In addition, New Guise makes a poor argument from analogy. Horses and wives are not much alike. Even if New Guise were correct that overfeeding causes spiritedness in wives (it doesn't), it does not follow that overfeeding causes spiritedness in horses.

New Guise thinks that overfeeding causes spiritedness in wives. Presumably, he would think that underfeeding would cause obedience in wives. The anonymous author of *The Taming of a Shrew* would agree.

In this society, a good wife is an obedient wife.

Ephesians 5:22-24 (King James Version) states:

22 Wives, submit yourselves unto your own husbands, as unto the Lord.

23 For the husband is the head of the wife, even as Christ is the head of the church: and he is the savior of the body.

24 Therefore as the church is subject unto Christ, so let the wives be [that is, submit] to their own husbands in everything.

"Where is this fellow speaking from?" Mankind asked. "Won't he come near?"

Mercy said:

"All too soon he will come, my brother, I fear, for your sake.

"He was here just now — I say this by Him Who ransomed me at a dear cost — with some of his fellows; they know and can cause much sorrow.

"They will be here very soon, if I go out.

"Think on my doctrine; it shall be your defense. Learn while I am here; set my words in your heart. Within a short space of time, I must necessarily go from here."

Nowadays said:

"The sooner the better, even if you leave right now! I believe that your name is Dolittle, you are so long from home.

"If you would go hence, we shall come, everyone, more than a large company of people. You have permission, I dare well say, when you want to, to go forth on your way. Men have little pleasure in your play because you make no entertainment: You are not amusing."

Nought said:

"Your broth shall get entirely cold, sir. When will you go dine?

"I have seen a man who lost twenty nobles [gold coins] at gambling in as little time. Yet it was not I, by Saint Quentin, for I was never worth a potful of cabbage since I was born."

Saint Quentin is the patron saint of prisoners.

Nought continued:

"My name is Nought. I love well to make merry. I have been before now with the common tapster of Bury St. Edmund's, and I have played the fool so long that I am weary."

A tapster is a bartender, but some tapsters, including female tapsters, had bad reputations. A "common woman" is a promiscuous woman or a prostitute.

Nought continued:

"Yet I shall be there again tomorrow."

New Guise, Nowadays, and Nought exited.

Mercy said to Mankind:

"I have much concern for you, my own friend. Your enemies will be here soon, they make their boast.

"Think well in your heart that your name is Mankind. Don't be unnatural to God. I ask you to be his servant.

"Be steadfast in your behavior; see that you are not variant and changeable. Don't lose through folly that which is bought so dear. God will test you soon; and if you are loyal to God, you shall be a perpetual sharer of His perpetual bliss.

"You may not have your intent at your first desire.

"See the great patience of Job in tribulation. Just as the blacksmith refines iron in the fire, so was Job tried by God's visitation of trials upon him.

"Job was of your human nature and of your fragility and frailty. Follow the steps of Job, my own sweet son, and in your trouble and adversity say as he said: *Dominus dedit, Dominus abstulit; sicut sibi placuit, ita factum est; nomen Domini benedictum!*"

The Latin means: The Lord gave, the Lord took away. As it pleased the Lord, so it was done. Blessed be the name of the Lord.

Job 1:20-21 (King James Version) states:

20 Then Job arose, and rent [tore] his mantle, and shaved his head, and fell down upon the ground, and worshipped,

21 And said, Naked came I out of my mother's womb, and naked shall I return thither: the Lord gave, and the Lord hath taken away; blessed be the name of the Lord.

Mercy continued:

"Moreover, I specially give you the responsibility to do this: Beware of New Guise, Nowadays, and Nought.

"Fashionable in their dress, they are boastful and loose in language. They shall seek all means to pervert your behavior.

"Good son, don't enter yourself in their company. They have not heard a mass this past year, I dare well say.

"Give them no audience: Don't listen to them. They will tell you many a lie.

"Do truly your labor and keep your holy day: the Sabbath and the religious festivals.

"Beware of Titivillus, for he misses no opportunity to tempt you. He goes about invisible and will not be seen. He will whisper in your ear and cast a net before your eye. He is the worst of them all. May God never let him prosper!"

Titivillus is the Devil: He is all vile things.

Mercy continued:

"If you displease God, ask for mercy immediately, or else Mischief will be ready to fasten you in his bridle.

"Kiss me now, my dear darling."

Mankind kissed Mercy.

Mercy continued:

"May God shield and guard you from your foes!

"Do truly your labor and be never idle. May the blessing of God be with you and with all these worshipful men and women!"

By "all these worshipful men and women," Mercy meant you: the audience.

Mercy exited.

Mankind said:

"Amen, for holy charity, amen!

"Now blessed be Jesus! My soul is well satisfied with the mellifluous and sweet doctrine of this worshipful man. The rebellion of my flesh now is overcome, thanks be to God that I came here and for the knowledge that I have acquired.

"Here I will sit and write on this paper the incomparable estate of my promised bliss."

Mankind wrote, and then Mankind said:

"Worshipful sovereigns, I have written here the glorious remembrance of my noble state.

"So that I may have remorse and memory of myself, thus it is written, in order to defend me from all superstitious charms:

"*Memento, homo, quod cinis es et in cinerem reverteris.*"

These words are used in Ash Wednesday services.

The Latin means: Remember, man, that you are dust and to dust you will return.

Job 34:15 states, "*All flesh shall perish together, and man shall turn again unto dust*" (King James Version).

Genesis 3:19 states, "*In the sweat of thy face shalt thou eat bread, till thou return unto the ground; for out of it wast thou taken: for dust thou art, and unto dust shalt thou return*" (King James Version).

A *memento mori* is a reminder of death: Someday each of us will die.

Mankind continued:

"Lo, I bear on my breast the badge of my arms."

Mankind's arms are his metaphorical coat of arms. He was perhaps wearing a cross on his chest.

A medieval custom was to write a Biblical verse and wear it hanging from the person's neck as a kind of charm. Mankind's arms included the words he had written down. If he kept those words in his mind, it would help protect him from temptation.

New Guise entered the scene.

He said:

"The weather is cold. May God send us good ferys!"

"Ferys" means 1) fires, and 2) feres — companions.

"*Cum sancto sanctus eris et cum perverso perverteris.*"

The Latin means: With the holy you will be holy, and with the corrupt you will be corrupted."

Psalm 18:25-26 (King James Version) states:

25 With the merciful thou wilt shew thyself merciful; with an upright man thou wilt shew thyself upright;

26 With the pure thou wilt shew thyself pure; and with the froward thou wilt shew thyself froward.

"Froward" means "perverse."

New Guise continued:

"*Ecce quam bonum et quam jocundum*, said the devil to the friars, *habitare fratres in unum.*"

The Latin means: Behold, how good and how agreeable that brothers should live together in unity."

Psalm 133.1 states, "*Behold, how good and how pleasant it is for brethren to dwell together in unity!*" (King James Version).

Mankind said:

"I hear a fellow speak; I will not mix with him.

"I shall start digging this earth with my spade. To avoid idleness, I do it my own self. I pray that God send it His plenty!"

Nowadays and Nought entered the scene, walking through the audience.

"Make room, sirs, for we have been away a long time," Nowadays said. "We will come give you a Christmas song."

Nought said:

"Now I ask all the yeomanry — all the folk — who are here to sing with us with a merry cheer."

Nought sang one line of the song at a time, and New Guise and Nowadays led the members of the audience, including you, in singing that line.

Nought sang:

"*It is written with a coal; it is written with a coal.*"

New Guise and Nowadays sang:

"*It is written with a coal; it is written with a coal.*"

Nought sang:

"*He that shitteth with his hole; he that shitteth with his hole.*"

New Guise and Nowadays sang:

"*He that shitteth with his hole; he that shitteth with his hole.*"

Nought sang:

"*Unless he wipe his arse clean; unless he wipe his arse clean.*"

New Guise and Nowadays sang:

"*Unless he wipe his arse clean; unless he wipe his arse clean.*"

Nought sang:

"*On his trousers it shall be seen; on his trousers it shall be seen.*"

New Guise and Nowadays sang:

"*On his trousers it shall be seen; on his trousers it shall be seen.*"

Nought, New Guise, and Nowadays sang:

"Holyke Holyke Holyke! Holyke Holyke Holyke!"

"Holyke!" means 1) Hole-lick! and 2) Hole-like! It is a perverted way of saying "Holy!"

New Guise said:

"Aye, Mankind, may God help you with your spade!

"I shall tell you about a marriage: I wish that your mouth and the arse of the man who made this song were married jointly together."

Mankind said:

"Get you hence, fellows, with reproach. Stop your derision, and stop your mocking.

"I must necessarily labor; it is my living."

Nowadays said:

"What, sir! We just got here!

"Shall all this corn grow here that you shall have the next year?

"If it shall be so, corn had better be expensive so you can sell it at a good price or else you shall have a poor life."

Nought said:

"Alas, good father, this labor wears you to the bone. But as for your crop, I take great moan and feel much sorrow.

"You shall never finish it alone. I shall try to get you a wife.

"How many acres do you estimate to be here?"

"Aye, how you turn the earth up and down!" New Guise said. "I have been in my days in many good towns, yet I never saw such another tilling."

"Why do you stand idle?" Mankind said. "It is a pity that you were born!"

"We shall bargain with you and neither mock nor scorn," Nowadays said. "Take a good cart in harvest and load it with your corn, and what shall we give you for what's left?"

Literally, Mankind did the work of raising the corn, and so he would get the corn.

Literally, Nought, New Guise, and Nowadays did no work, and so they would get what was left, which would be at most chaff and straw.

But Nought, New Guise, and Nowadays wanted Mankind to figuratively get rid of his corn and to figuratively become chaff and straw like Nought, New Guise, and Nowadays.

Nought said:

"He is a good strong laborer; he would gladly do well.

"He has met with the good man Mercy in a shrewd sell."

A "shrewd sell" is a "cunning con." Nought would say that Mankind has been conned into working very hard for very little.

In one way, this is true. Adam and Eve did not need to labor in the Garden of Eden. Once the serpent (Satan) conned Adam and Eve into sinning, they had to leave the Garden of Eden and they had to labor.

Genesis 3:16-19 (King James Version) states:

16 Unto the woman he [God] said, I will greatly multiply thy sorrow and thy conception; in sorrow thou shalt bring forth children; and thy desire shall be to thy husband, and he shall rule over thee.

17 And unto Adam he [God] said, Because thou hast hearkened unto the voice of thy wife, and hast eaten of the tree, of which I commanded thee, saying, Thou shalt not eat of it: cursed is the ground for thy sake; in sorrow shalt thou eat of it all the days of thy life;

18 Thorns also and thistles shall it bring forth to thee; and thou shalt eat the herb of the field;

19 In the sweat of thy face shalt thou eat bread, till thou return unto the ground; for out of it wast thou taken: for dust thou art, and unto dust shalt thou return.

In another way, it is not true. Mankind's reward for his hard work now will be Paradise in the next life.

Mankind's "shrewd sell" was being conned by the serpent; Mercy did not con Mankind.

Nought, New Guise, and Nowadays wanted to con Mankind.

Nought continued:

"For all this he may have many a hungry [skimpy] meal. Yet you will see that he is politic and shrewd. Here shall be good corn, he cannot miss it.

"If he will have rain, he may piss over it, and if he will have compost, he may similarly bless it by spreading over it a little compost with his arse."

"Compost" is fertilizer; in this case, it is human manure.

Mankind said:

"Go and do your labor! May God let you never prosper.

"Or with my spade I shall strike you, by the Holy Trinity! Have you no other man to mock, but always you must mock me? You would have me be one of your gang?

"Hurry yourselves away from here lively, for I will drive you away from here."

Mankind beat Nought, New Guise, and Nowadays with his spade, wounding each of them.

New Guise said, "Alas, my family jewels! Ow, my testicles! I shall be in disgrace with my wife because of impotence."

Previously, New Guise's wife had wounded his head and his peson — his penis.

"Alas!" Nowadays said. "And I am likely never to thrive, for I have had such a blow."

Nowadays' head was wounded.

Mankind said:

"Go away, I say, New Guise, Nowadays, and Nought!

"It was said to me previously that all means should be sought to corrupt my behavior and bring me to nought.

"Go away, thieves! You have made many a lie."

Nought said:

"Marred — suffering — I was because of the cold weather, but now I am warm."

He was warm because Mankind had beaten him.

Nought continued:

"You are evilly advised, sir, for you have done harm. By Cock's [God's] sacred body, I have such a pain in my arm that I may not change — buy or sell — a man worth a farthing."

A farthing is a quarter penny.

Because of his arm injury, Nought cannot give a man change for a farthing. And because of his arm injury, Nought cannot charge a man even a farthing for any work Nought might do because Nought cannot work.

Because of his arm injury, Nought is incapacitated.

Nought, New Guise, and Nowadays started to leave.

Mankind knelt and said:

"Now I thank God, kneeling on my knee.

"Blessed be his name! He is of high degree. By the help of His grace that He has sent me, I have put to flight three of my enemies.

"Yet, sovereigns, this instrument — my spade — is not made to defend.

"David says, *Nec in hasta, nec in gladio, salvat Dominus.*"

The Latin means: Not with the spear, nor with the sword, the Lord saves.

In I Kings 17.47 (King James Version), David said to Goliath, "*And all this assembly shall know that the LORD saveth not with sword and spear: for the battle is the LORD's, and he will give you into our hands.*"

Over his shoulder while departing, Nought said:

"No, marry, I curse you, it is in spadibus."

"Marry" is a mild curse: By the Virgin Mary.

"Spadibus" is mock Latin for "spade."

Nought continued:

"Therefore, may Christ's curse come upon your hedibus to send you less might and strength!"

"Hedibus" is mock Latin for "head."

Nought, New Guise, and Nowadays exited.

Mankind said to you, the audience:

"I promise you that these fellows will come here no more, for some of them, certainly, were somewhat too near for their own good.

"My spiritual father, Mercy, advised me to be of a good cheer and to be confident and to fight manly against my enemies.

"I shall conquer them, I think — every one of them.

"Yet I say amiss — I am in error — for I don't do it alone. With the help of the grace of God, I resist my foes and their malicious hearts.

"With my spade I will depart, my worshipful sovereigns, and live always with labor to correct my pride.

"I will go fetch corn-seed for my land; I ask you to be patient. Very soon I shall return."

Mankind exited.

CHAPTER 2

— Scene 2 —

— Fall —

Mischief said:

"Alas, alas, that I was ever created! Alas the while, I am worse than nothing! Since I was here, I am utterly undone and ruined by Him Who redeemed me!"

Jesus suffered on the cross for all, but many persons (and demons) have rejected that redemption. In addition, Mercy has bested Mischief.

Mischief continued:

"I, Mischief, was here at the beginning of the game, and I argued with Mercy. May God give him shame! While I have been absent, Mercy has taught Mankind to fight manly against his foes.

"For with his spade, which was his weapon, he has thoroughly beaten New Guise, Nowadays, and Nought. I feel great pity to see them weep. Will you listen? I hear them cry."

Weeping and crying aloud, Nought, New Guise, and Nowadays entered the scene.

Mischief continued:

"Alas! Alas, come here, I shall be your protector. Alack! Alack! *Vene! Vene!*"

The Latin means: Come! Come!

Mischief continued:

"Come hither with sorrow! Peace, fair babes, you shall have an apple tomorrow!"

In other words: Things will be better tomorrow.

Mischief then asked:

"Why do you weep so? Why?"

New Guise said, "Alas, master, alas, my private parts!"

Mischief said:

"Ah, where? Alack! Fair babe, kiss me!"

New Guise started to pull his pants down.

Mischief quietly said:

"Abide! Stop! Too soon I shall see it."

"It" was something that he did not want to kiss.

Possibly, many of them are seen in Hell. In Dante's *Inferno*, all of the sinners except the Hypocrites are naked. The Hypocrites wear heavy cloaks that are iron on the inside and gold on the outside.

Nowadays said, "Here, here, see my head, good master!"

Mischief said, "Our Lady, help! Poor darling, *vene! Vene!* I shall help thee with thy pain; I shall smite off thy head and set it on again!"

Nought said:

"By Our Lady, sir, a 'fair' remedy!

"Will you cut off his head? It is a shrewd charm: a tough cure."

Yes, cutting off Nowadays' head will stop the pain.

Nought continued:

"As for me, I have no harm. I would be loathe to do without my arm. You play *in nomine patris*, chop!"

In other words, Mischief playfully — that is, mockingly — says a quick prayer — "in the name of the Father" — and then he starts amputating.

New Guise said, "You shall not chop off my jewels — my balls — if I can help it."

Nowadays said, "You, by Christ's cross, will you smite my head away? There! Where? One head and one body! Get out of here! You shall not try. I might be called a fool."

In other words: Nowadays did not want Mischief to chop him in two — head and body — because Nowadays would look foolish without his head.

"I can chop it off and make it on again," Mischief said.

New Guise said, "I have a shrewd *recumbentibus*, but I feel no pain."

The mock-Latin means: knock-down blow.

Nowadays said:

"And my head is all safe and whole again."

They were pretending to be OK so that Mischief would not start amputating things that they would miss.

Nowadays said to Mischief:

"Now touching on the matter of Mankind, let us have a discussion, since you have come here. It would be good to have an end to the matter."

They wanted to finish the business of convincing Mankind to change his behavior from good to bad.

They huddled together and talked.

One of the demons had the idea of bringing in the big gun: Titivillus. One way to attract him was with music.

Mischief said, "What! Now! A minstrel! Do you know any?"

Nought said, "I can pipe in a Walsingham whistle, I, Nought, Nought."

Perhaps he meant that he could play the flute, but not well.

At Walsingham was a shrine dedicated to the Virgin Mary. People made pilgrimages to it. Nought's whistle — his flute — came from there.

Mischief said, "Blow apace, and thou shall bring him in with a flute."

Nought played his flute.

Still out of sight, Titivillus called, "I come with my legs under me."

Mischief said, "Now, New Guise, Nowadays, listen to me before I go! When our heads were together, I spoke of *si dedero*."

The Latin means: If I will give.

The actors were going to ask audience members for money. If they contributed enough money, they would see the Devil: Titivillus.

New Guise said to Mischief:

"You, go thy way!"

The actor playing Mischief probably doubled as Titivillus, and so Mischief needed to exit.

New Guise added:

"We shall gather money for that purpose, or else there shall no man see him — Titivillus."

Please note that it took the anonymous author of *Mankind* a long time to go from talking about God to talking about dollars (and it's the demons who talk about money); in that respect the author is vastly the superior of many televised evangelical preachers.

Mischief exited.

New Guise said to the audience:

"Now devoutly to our purpose and business, worshipful sovereigns, we intend to gather money, if it pleases your negligence, for a man with a head that is of great power."

Contributing money to see the Devil might well be negligence of spiritual matters.

Nowadays said to New Guise:

"Keep your tally, in goodness I ask you, good brother!"

In other words: Keep track of how much money the audience gives to see Titivillus.

Nowadays then said:

"He is a worshipful man, sirs, saving your reverence.

"He loves no groats, nor pence or two pence.

"Give us red royals if you will see his abominable presence."

Titivillus was a devil who did not value small coins such as groats.

Red royals are gold coins.

New Guise said:

"Not so! You who may not pay the one, may pay the other."

Few, if any, audience members could afford to pay a gold coin. New Guise, for one, would welcome coins of less value than a red royal.

"First we will try the good-man — the host — of this inn."

New Guise collected a coin (or pretended to collect a coin) from the host and said, "God bless you, master! You may complain, yet you will not say nay."

The host may be complaining under his breath. Or New Guise may be pretending that the host was complaining under his breath.

He then said to Nowadays and Nought:

"Let us go by and by and make them pay one by one."

They collected money from the audience.

Readers can use PayPal to send money to David Bruce at — nah, I'm not going to do that to you. But the final appendix of this book is "Some Books by David Bruce." That is David Bruce's version of making audience members exit through the gift shop.

New Guide then said:

"All of you pay! May all of you have good luck!"

Nought said, "I say, New Guise, Nowadays, *estis vos pecuniatus*? I have cried for money a fair amount of time. I curse your heads!"

The Latin means: Are you rich? Are you in the money?

Nowadays said to the out-of-sight Titivillus:

"*Ita vere, magister.*"

The Latin means: So truly, master.

In other words: We have enough money for you to appear.

He then said to Titivillus:

"Come forth now from out of your gate!"

He then said to the audience:

"He is a goodly man, sirs; make space and beware!"

Wearing a horrible mask, Titivillus entered the scene.

He said to the audience:

"*Ego sum dominancium dominus*, and my name is Titivillus."

The Latin means: I am lord of lords.

Deuteronomy 10:17 states, "*For the Lord your God is God of gods, and Lord of lords, a great God, a mighty, and a terrible, which regardeth not persons, nor taketh reward:*" (King James Version).

Revelation 19:16 states, "*And he hath on his vesture and on his thigh a name written, King Of Kings, And Lord Of Lords*" (King James Version).

Titivillus continued:

"You who have good horses, to you I say, *Caveatis*!"

The Latin means: Beware!

Titivillus continued:

"Here is a fellowship able to entice them out of your gates!

"*Ego probo sic.*"

The Latin means: Thus I prove it.

Titivillus said to New Guise:

"Sir New Guise, lend me a penny!"

New Guise said:

"I have a large purse, sir, but I have no money. By the mass, I am two farthings short of a halfpenny."

A halfpenny is two farthings, so New Guise had no money in his purse. Well, so he claimed. He actually had just collected money from the audience.

New Guise continued:

"Yet I had ten pounds last night."

He had probably lost it drinking and gambling.

Titivillus said to Nowadays, "What is in thy purse? Thou are a valiant fellow."

Nowadays said:

"The devil have the lot! The devil can have all I have! I am a clean gentleman."

"Clean" can mean "pure," but Nowadays meant "penniless."

Nowadays continued:

"I pray to God that I am never worse stored with money than I am right now. It shall be otherwise, I hope, before this night has passed."

Nowadays had also just collected money from the audience.

Titivillus said to Nought, "Listen to me, now! I say thou have many a penny."

Nought said:

"*Non nobis, domine! Non nobis!* By Saint Denny!"

The Latin means: Not to us, Lord! Not to us!

Psalm 115:1 stated, "*Not unto us, O Lord, not unto us, but unto thy name give glory, for thy mercy, and for thy truth's sake*" (King James Version).

Saint Denis is the patron saint of the French monarchy.

Nought continued:

"The devil may dance in my purse for any penny I have. It is as clean as a bird's arse."

Titivillus went to the three other demons and revealed the money that they collected.

Titivillus said to the audience:

"Now I say yet again, *Caveatis!* Beware!

"Here is a fellowship able to entice your horse from out of your gates."

He then said:

"Now I say, New Guise, Nowadays, and Nought, go and search the country. Immediately, let it be searched. Some search here, some search there. See if you may catch and steal anything. If you fail to steal a horse, steal whatever else you can."

New Guise said, "Then speak to Mankind about the recumbentibus — the knock-down blow — to my jewels."

Nowadays said, "Remember my broken head in the worship of the five vowels."

This is a demon's way of referring to the five wounds Christ suffered on the cross.

Nought said, "Yes, good sir, and talk to Mankind about the sciatica in my arm."

Sciatica is a pain that affects the lower half of the body.

Titivillus said to the demons:

"I know very well what Mankind did to you.

"Mischief has thoroughly informed me about the matter.

"I shall avenge your quarrel, I vow to God.

"Go forth, and see where you may do harm. Take Donald Trump to help you, if you will have another companion.

"I say, New Guise, to where are thou determined to go?"

New Guise said:

"First I shall begin with former Speaker of the House Kevin McCarthy of California.

"From there I shall go forth to United States Representative Marjorie Greene of Georgia, and then I will go forth to United States Representative Lauren Boebert of Colorado.

"I will keep myself to these three."

Actually, any high-ranking United States politician would be a good mark for these demons. In the United States, high-ranking politicians tend to be very wealthy. In the United States, public servants tend to have a lot of servants. Still, Republican politicians tend to help the wealthy become wealthier by giving them tax breaks and lax regulations, and so Republican politicians ought to have a lot to steal.

Being evil, demons have no trouble preying on their own.

Matthew 6:24 states, "*No man can serve two masters: for either he will hate the one, and love the other; or else he will hold to the one, and despise the other. Ye cannot serve God and mammon*" (King James Version).

Nowadays said:

"I shall go to Minority Leader of the United States Senate Mitch McConnell of Kentucky and to United States Representative George Santos of Atlantis.

"I shall spare President Joe Biden. He is a *noli me tangere*."

The Latin means: Do not touch me.

John 20:17 states, "*Jesus saith unto her, Touch me not; for I am not yet ascended to my Father: but go to my brethren, and say unto them, I ascend unto my Father, and your Father; and to my God, and your God*" (King James Version).

Nought said:

"I shall go to Joel Osteen of Texas.

"I shall spare Pope Francis of Rome and the volunteers who work at the local food bank, for dread of *in manus tuas* — crack!"

The Latin states: "into your hands."

The "crack" was that of a neck being broken on the gallows.

Luke 23:46 states, "*And when Jesus had cried with a loud voice, he said, Father, into thy hands I commend my spirit: and having said thus, he gave up the ghost*" (King James Version).

People will fight to protect Pope Francis and the volunteers who work at the local food bank. Or if not, they ought to,

Nought continued:

"Fellows, come forth, and we will go away from here together."

New Guise said, "Since we shall go, let us be well aware where we are going. If we should be arrested, we will come back here no more. Let us learn well our neck verse, so that we will not have a check."

A neck verse was a short passage of scripture in Latin. Priests knew Latin, and if a person could read Latin, they could escape hanging by being tried in an ecclesiastical court.

Titivillus said:

"Go on your way, a devil's way, go on your way, all of you!

"I bless you with my left hand: May foul luck befall you!"

Priests bless with the right hand.

Titivillus continued:

"Come again, I warn you, as soon as I call you, and bring your booty to this place."

Everyone except Titivillus exited.

Alone, Titivillus said:

"To speak with Mankind, I will stay here at this time and try to get him to set aside his good purpose. The good man Mercy shall no longer be his guide. I shall make him dance another dance.

"Always I go about invisible to human eyes; it is my fashion. And before his eye thus I will hang my net to blind his sight; I hope to take his measure and find out what kind of man he is."

The Devil carries a net to use to trap sinners.

Titivillus continued:

"To irk him about his labor, I shall make a trick. This board shall be hidden under the earth secretly. His spade shall enter the earth, I hope, unreadily."

Titivillus buried the board in the soil.

He continued:

"By the time he has attempted to turn over the earth so he can plant his seed, he shall be very angry and he will lose his patience with the pain of shame.

"I shall mix his corn-seed with the seeds of cockle and darnel: two kinds of weed.

"His corn-seed shall not be fit to sow nor shall his corn be fit to sell."

This calls to mind the Parable of the Sower in Matthew 13:24-30 (King James Version):

24 Another parable put he forth unto them, saying, The kingdom of heaven is likened unto a man which sowed good seed in his field:

25 But while men slept, his enemy came and sowed tares among the wheat, and went his way.

26 But when the blade was sprung up, and brought forth fruit, then appeared the tares also.

27 So the servants of the householder came and said unto him, Sir, didst not thou sow good seed in thy field? from whence then hath it tares?

28 He said unto them, An enemy hath done this. The servants said unto him, Wilt thou then that we go and gather them up?

29 But he said, Nay; lest while ye gather up the tares, ye root up also the wheat with them.

30 Let both grow together until the harvest: and in the time of harvest I will say to the reapers, Gather ye together first the tares, and bind them in bundles to burn them: but gather the wheat into my barn.

It also calls to mind the Parable of the Tares of the Field in Matthew 13:36-43 (King James Version)

36 Then Jesus sent the multitude away, and went into the house: and his disciples came unto him, saying, Declare unto us the parable of the tares of the field.

37 He answered and said unto them, He that soweth the good seed is the Son of man;

38 The field is the world; the good seed are the children of the kingdom; but the tares are the children of the wicked one;

39 The enemy that sowed them is the devil; the harvest is the end of the world; and the reapers are the angels.

40 As therefore the tares are gathered and burned in the fire; so shall it be in the end of this world.

41 The Son of man shall send forth his angels, and they shall gather out of his kingdom all things that offend, and them which do iniquity;

42 And shall cast them into a furnace of fire: there shall be wailing and gnashing of teeth.

43 Then shall the righteous shine forth as the sun in the kingdom of their Father. Who hath ears to hear, let him hear.

Titivillus continued:

"Yonder he comes. I ask you to keep my plan secret.

"He shall think that grace is lacking."

Carrying seed-corn, Mankind entered the scene.

He said, "Now may God of His mercy send us of his guidance. I have brought seed here to sow my land with. While I dig over my land, here my seed-corn shall stand."

Mankind put down his seed-corn.

Invisible to Mankind, Titivillus took the seed-corn and said, "*In nomine Patris et Filii et Spiritus Sancti*, now I will begin."

The Latin means: In the name of the Father, the Son, and the Holy Spirit.

Titivillus then carried away the seed-corn.

Attempting but failing to turn over the soil so he could plant it, Mankind said:

"This land is so hard it makes me tired and irritated.

"I shall sow my corn at winter and let God work."

Winter wheat does exist in some areas, but the seeds are sown in the autumn in the northern hemisphere. The wheat is dormant during the winter and begins growing in early spring. The result is an early harvest.

Mankind looked for his seed-corn, but he could not find it.

He said:

"Alas, my corn is lost! Here is a foul work!

"I see well that by tilling I shall win little. Here I give up my spade now and forever."

Mankind put down his spade. Invisible, Titivillus picked up the spade and carried it away.

Mankind then said:

"To occupy my body, I will not put myself to work.

"I will hear my evensong — vespers — here before I leave. This place I assign for my church. Here in my church, I kneel on my knees."

Evensong consists of prayers and hymns.

He prayed:

"*Pater noster qui es in celis.*"

The Latin is the beginning of the Lord's Prayer: Our Father Who is in Heaven."

Prayers can be said anywhere and can be said by a lone person, but there are advantages to praying in a church with other believers.

Returning to the scene, still invisible, Titivillus said to you, the audience:

"I promise you I have no lead on my heels. I am here again to make this fellow irritated.

"Hush! Peace! I shall go to his ear and whisper in it."

He whispered:

"A short prayer pierces Heaven; cease thy prayer. Thou are holier than ever was any of thy kin.

"Arise and relieve thyself. Nature compels you to relieve thyself."

Mankind said to you, the audience:

"I will go into this yard, sovereigns, and come back again soon. For dread of the colic [intestinal and stomach problems] and also of the kidney stone and gall stone, I will go do that which necessarily must be done.

"My prayer-beads shall be here for whosoever wants them."

Mankind may have meant: for whoever wants to use them for a little while.

Leaving his prayer-beads behind, Mankind exited.

Titivillus said:

"Mankind was busy in his prayer, yet I made him arise.

"He is distracted — by Christ! — from his divine service.

"Where is he, do you think? Indeed, I am wonderfully wise. I have sent him forth to shit his loss."

Mankind was distracted from his religious duty and so he was losing the chance to commune with God.

Titivillus continued:

"If you have any silver, perhaps pure brass, take a little powder of Paris and cast it over its face, and then in the owl-flight — the twilight — it will pass."

Titivillus was teaching you a way to counterfeit money. This would make a brass coin pass as a silver coin in the dark. The counterfeit coin would not pass in the daytime.

This is a poor way to counterfeit money. As soon as daylight comes, the victim will know that he or she has been conned.

Titivillus had also taught the audience how to counterfeit holiness. He had done this by telling Mankind, "A short prayer pierces Heaven; cease thy prayer. Thou are holier than ever was any of thy kin."

He had flattered Mankind by calling him "holier than ever was any of thy kin," and he had told Mankind that his prayer was so effective that it need not be long — therefore, stop praying.

Titivillus continued:

"Titivillus can teach you many clever things.

"Mankind will come again soon, or else I fear that evensong will be finished."

Titivillus was pretending to worry that Mankind might miss hearing vespers.

He continued:

"His prayer-beads shall be cast aside for good, and that soon.

"You in the audience shall have a good entertainment if you will abide and stay here."

He looked up and said:

"Mankind comes again! May he fare well! I shall answer him *ad omnia quare*: I shall answer him *at every why*.

"There shall be set in action a clerical, learned matter: a controversy. I hope to set him aside from his purpose."

Controversies can keep people away from religion.

Mankind said:

"Evensong has been in the saying, I think, a fair while.

"I am irritated by it; it is too long by one mile. Enough of that! I will no more go so often over the church stile. Be as be may, I shall do otherwise.

"I am irritated by both labor and prayer. I want no more of it, although Mercy will be angry. My head is very heavy, I tell you truly. I shall sleep my bellyful even if Mercy were my brother."

Mankind lay down and slept.

Titivillus said to you, the audience:

"If ever you did, for me keep now your silence. Not a word, I charge you, on pain of forfeiture of forty pence. A pretty game shall be shown to you before you go away from here.

"You may hear Mankind snore; he is sound asleep.

"Hush! Peace! The devil is dead."

When the devil is dead, all is well: An enemy has been overcome. In this case, the enemy was Mercy. Titivillus felt confident that he could turn Mankind to evil. After all, Mankind was asleep when he should have been awake.

Titivillus continued:

"I shall go whisper in Mankind's ear."

He whispered:

"Alas, Mankind, alas! Mercy has stolen a mare. He has run away from his master; no man knows where. Moreover, he stole both a horse and a cow.

"But yet I heard that he broke his neck as he rode in France. But I think he rides on the gallows, in order to learn how to dance at the end of a rope, because of his theft: That is his punishment. Trust him no more, for he is a marred and married man."

Catholic priests are not supposed to marry.

Titivillus continued:

"You wrought — made — much sorrow with thy spade previously. Arise and ask for mercy from New Guise, Nowadays, and Nought. They can advise thee for the best; let their good will be sought.

"And deceive thine own wife, and take to thee a lover."

Titivillus addressed the audience:

"Farewell, everyone! For I have done my game because I have brought Mankind to mischief and to shame."

Titivillus exited, and Mankind awoke.

Mankind said:

"Whoop-who! Whoop-who!"

He was ready to party and act like one of Jonathan Swift's Yahoos from Book 4 of *Gulliver's Travels*.

Thinking that he had dreamed and that the dream was true, Mankind continued:

"Mercy has broken his neck-kerchief, they say, or he hangs by the neck high upon the gallows."

He said to you, the audience:

"Adieu, fair masters! I will go to the ale house and speak with New Guise, Nowadays, and Nought. And I will get myself a mistress with a kissable face."

Wearing a noose around his neck, New Guise ran as he entered the scene.

He said:

"Make room, for Cock's [God's] sacred body, make room! Aha! Well over-run!"

In his haste, New Guise had almost run into Mankind and knocked him down.

New Guise continued:

"May God give him — the hangman — evil luck! We were near Saint Patrick's way, I swear by Him Who redeemed me."

Saint Patrick is the patron saint of Ireland. When he was sixteen, he was captured by Irish pirates and made a slave.

Saint Patrick's Purgatory was a pilgrimage site in County Donegal, Ireland. It was a cave that was reputed to be an entrance to Purgatory.

The demons had run into trouble very quickly.

New Guise continued:

"I was jerked by the neck; the game of hanging was begun.

"A grace was that the noose — the hanging rope — broke in two."

He pointed to the noose around his neck and said, "*Ecce signum*!"

The Latin means: Behold the sign!"

John 20:19-20 (King James Version) states:

19 Then the same day at evening, being the first day of the week, when the doors were shut where the disciples were assembled for fear of the Jews, came Jesus and stood in the midst, and saith unto them, Peace be unto you.

20 And when he had so said, he shewed unto them his hands and his side. Then were the disciples glad, when they saw the Lord.

John 20:24-31 (King James Version) states:

24 But Thomas, one of the twelve, called Didymus, was not with them when Jesus came.

25 The other disciples therefore said unto him, We have seen the Lord. But he said unto them, Except I shall see in his hands the print of the nails, and put my finger into the print of the nails, and thrust my hand into his side, I will not believe.

26 And after eight days again his disciples were within, and Thomas with them: then came Jesus, the doors being shut, and stood in the midst, and said, Peace be unto you.

27 Then saith he to Thomas, Reach hither thy finger, and behold my hands; and reach hither thy hand, and thrust it into my side: and be not faithless, but believing.

28 And Thomas answered and said unto him, My Lord and my God.

29 Jesus saith unto him, Thomas, because thou hast seen me, thou hast believed: blessed are they that have not seen, and yet have believed.

30 And many other signs truly did Jesus in the presence of his disciples, which are not written in this book:

31 But these are written, that ye might believe that Jesus is the Christ, the Son of God; and that believing ye might have life through his name.

New Guise continued:

"The half is about my neck; we had a near run — a narrow escape!

"'Beware,' said the good-wife when she smote off her husband's head. 'Beware!'

"Mischief is a convict, for he could recite his neck-verse."

Mischief had been able to read some Scripture in Latin, and so he had escaped being hung, but he was in prison.

New Guise continued:

"My body gave a swing when I hung upon the gibbet. Alas, the hangman will hang such an attractive and fierce man as me for the stealing of a horse — I pray that God gives him sorrow!"

New Guise said to you, the audience:

"Take off this noose! What the devil is Mankind doing here, I say with sorrow!"

Earlier, Mankind had beaten New Guise with a spade.

New Guise said:

"Alas, how sore my neck is, I say!"

He took off the noose.

Mankind said, "You are welcome, New Guise! Sir, how are you?"

"Well, sir, I have no cause to mourn," New Guise said.

Mankind asked, "What was that around your neck, so God you amend?"

God is a healer, and New Guise needed to be healed.

Matthew 5:45 states, "*That ye may be the children of your Father which is in heaven: for he maketh his sun to rise on the evil and on the good, and sendeth rain on the just and on the unjust*" (King James Version).

God will heal good people and bad people.

"So may God reform you," aka "So God you amend," may be a polite way of saying "please," but many people reform when facing death.

New Guise said:

"In faith, it was Saint Audrey's holy band."

Saint Audrey is the patron saint of throat and neck complaints.

New Guise continued:

"I have a little disease, as it pleased God to send, with a running ringworm."

Ringworm is an itchy fungal skin infection. It is contagious and forms a ring-shaped pattern.

New Guise's "ringworm" consisted of the marks the noose made around his neck.

New Guise was pretending that the noose was a neckband that he had gotten from a shrine dedicated to Saint Audrey: a neckband that he was wearing as a treatment for disease.

Running ringworm is oozing ringworm.

"Running" also refers to the running that New Guise engaged in to escape from being hung.

Carrying items, including sacramental wafers and wine, that he had stolen from a church, Nowadays entered the scene. He had other items that he could sell for money.

Nowadays said:

"Make room, I ask thee, my brother! I have labored all this night. When shall we go dine?"

Luke 5:5 states, "*And Simon answering said unto him, Master, we have toiled all the night, and have taken nothing: nevertheless at thy word I will let down the net*" (King James Version).

Nowadays continued:

"A church near here shall pay for the ale, bread, and wine. Look, here is stuff that will serve to feed us."

New Guise said, "Now by the holy Mary, thou are a better merchant than I!"

Nought entered the scene.

Seeing the sacramental wafers, he said, "Get out of the way, knaves, let me go by! If I can't get some of that food, I will starve."

This is spiritually true of many people, but they need to partake of that food and drink worthily.

1 Corinthians 11:24-29 (King James Version) states:

24 And when he had given thanks, he brake it, and said, Take, eat: this is my body, which is broken for you: this do in remembrance of me.

25 After the same manner also he took the cup, when he had supped, saying, this cup is the new testament in my blood: this do ye, as oft as ye drink it, in remembrance of me.

26 For as often as ye eat this bread, and drink this cup, ye do shew the Lord's death till he come.

27 Wherefore whosoever shall eat this bread, and drink this cup of the Lord, unworthily, shall be guilty of the body and blood of the Lord.

28 But let a man examine himself, and so let him eat of that bread, and drink of that cup.

29 For he that eateth and drinketh unworthily, eateth and drinketh damnation to himself, not discerning the Lord's body.

Nought munched the sacramental wafers.

Mischief entered the scene. He was carrying broken shackles.

He said:

"Here comes a man of arms! Why do you stand so still? Why are you surprised? I have my belly-full of murder and manslaughter."

"What! Mischief, have you been in prison?" Nowadays said. "If it is your will, it seems to me that you have scored — broken — a pair of fetters."

Mischief said:

"I was chained by the arms. Look, I have the chains here.

"The chains I burst asunder and killed the jailer. Yes, and I embraced his fair wife in a corner. Ah, how sweetly I kissed that sweet mouth of hers!"

This kind of "embrace" is likely a rape.

Mischief continued:

"When I had finished, I was my own butler. I brought away with me both dish and platter. Here is enough for me; be of good cheer! Yet may the new venture fare well!"

Mankind knelt and said, "I ask for mercy from New Guise, Nowadays, and Nought. I remember that I fought you once with my spade. I will make you amends if I hurt you in any way at all or did any grievance to you."

"Why the devil do thou want to be of this disposition?" New Guise asked. "Why have you changed your mind about us?"

Mankind said:

"I dreamed that Mercy was hanged: This was my vision. And I dreamed that I should have recourse and resort to you three.

"Now I ask you heartily for your good will and friendship — I ask you for mercy of all that I did amiss."

"I say, New Guise and Nought, that Titivillus did all this," Nowadays said. "As surely as God is in Heaven, so this is true."

Nought said to Mankind:

"Stand up on your feet!"

Mankind arose.

Nought then said to Mankind:

"Why do you stand so still and motionless?"

Nought may have been sarcastic. Mankind may have been trembling in despair.

After all, Mankind was breaking bad: He was deciding to turn evil. He believed that Mercy had turned evil and had stolen a mare, a horse, and a cow, and then had been hanged for it.

If Mercy turns evil, what hope is there for the rest of us?

New Guise said:

"Master Mischief, we will exhort you to write down Mankind's name in your book of loyal followers."

Mischief decided not to do that yet. First a manor-court session needed to be held to see if Mankind qualified.

Mischief said:

"I will not do so; instead, I will set a manor-court.

"Nowadays, make proclamation, and do it *sub forma iuris*, fool!"

The Latin means: in the proper legal form.

Nowadays proclaimed:

"Oyez! Oyez! Oyez! All manner of men and common women, listen!"

"Oyez!" means "Be quiet and pay attention!" "Common women" are promiscuous women and whores.

Nowadays continued:

"To the court of Mischief either come or send thy excuse!

"Mankind shall retorn and return; he is of our men."

Original sin had been committed in the Garden of Eden. Now Mankind was ready to sin again and return to evil.

Mischief said, "Nought, come forward. Thou shall be the steward."

Nought would record the trial.

New Guise said about Mankind's coat, "Master Mischief, his side gown — the bottom of his long coat — may be sold. He may have a jacket instead, and money to count."

New Guise would cut off the bottom of the long coat and make it a short jacket. The cut-off cloth would be sold.

Mankind took off his long coat and said:

"I will do what's for the best, as long as I get no cold."

A short jacket would not keep him warm in winter.

He said to New Guise:

"Wait a moment, I ask you, and take it with you. And let me have it again in any form."

New Guise took the long coat and said, "I promise you a fresh jacket after the new guise: the new fashion."

Mankind said, "Go, and do that which pertains to your duty, and save what cloth you can."

A long coat is warm in winter. Short jackets are not as warm.

Coats were important possessions in the Middle Ages and in other ages. Often, impoverished people had no coats.

St. Francis of Assisi and a friend named Giles were out walking when they came across a beggar woman. St. Francis had nothing to give her, as he was wearing a simple, much-worn habit with a bit of rope for a belt. Giles, however, was wearing a coat. St. Francis told him, "Give it to her." Giles handed the beggar woman the coat, and he became one of the first Franciscans.

New Guise exited.

Nought wrote something and then said, "Wait, master Mischief, and read this."

Mischief said:

"Here is —"

He read out loud:

"*Blottibus in blottis.*

"*Blottorum blottibus istis.*"

Writing was done with a goose-quill pen that was dipped in ink. Dripping ink sometimes created blots.

Mischief then said:

"I curse your ears, a 'fair' handwriting!"

Nowadays said, "Yes, it is a good running fist: a good cursive handwriting. Such a handwriting may not be missed."

Such bad handwriting needed to be seen to be believed.

"I would have done better, had I known how to," Nought said.

Mischief said:

"Take heed, sirs, it stood you on hand — it behooves you."

Mischief read out loud:

"*Curia tenta generalis ...*"

The Latin meant:

"The general court having been held ..."

Mischief said:

"In a place where good ale is."

Mischief read out loud:

"*Anno regni regitalis Edwardi nullateni ...*"

The Latin meant: In the regnal year of Edward the None.

Looking at Nought's writing, Mischief said:

"On yesterday in Feverer [February]."

Mischief then said:

"The year has completely passed, as Nought has written."

Nought had written the wrong day and the wrong month. Or Mischief regarded March 1 as the start of the new year.

March was the first month in the early Roman calendar. This was in pagan times. Around 700 B.C.E. January and February were added to the calendar.

Mischief said sarcastically:

"Nought here is our Tully Cicero."

Marcus Tullius Cicero was a master of Latin composition.

Mischief then read out loud:

"— *anno regni regis nulli!*"

The Latin means: in the regnal year of no king.

Seeing New Guise coming, Nowadays said, "How are things now, New Guise? Thou make much delay. That jacket shall not be worth a farthing."

New Guise entered the scene. He was carrying Mankind's coat, which had been shortened.

He said:

"Out of my way, sirs, for fear of fighting!

"Look, here is a neat cut, which makes it easy to leap about!"

Nought said about Mankind's coat:

"Its shape is not worth a morsel of bread. There is too much cloth; it weighs as heavy as does lead.

"I shall go and mend it, or else I will lose my head. Make room, sirs. Let me go out."

Nought exited, carrying Mankind's coat.

Mischief said:

"Mankind, come here! May God send you the gout!"

Gout can be caused by a rich diet and excess weight.

Mischief continued:

"You shall go to all the good fellows in the country round about here, and you will go to the good-wife when the good-man — the husband — is out.

"'I will,' say ye."

"I will, sir," Mankind said.

Nowadays said:

"There are only six deadly sins; lechery is not one of them, as may be verified by us villains, every one of us.

"You shall go rob, steal, and kill, as fast as you may go.

"'I will,' say you."

"I will, sir," Mankind said.

Nowadays said:

"On Sundays in the morning at a good time, you shall go with us to the ale-house early to dine.

"And you will miss mass and matins, canonical hours, and prime."

These are times for prayers.

Nowadays continued:

"'I will,' say you."

"I will, sir," Mankind said.

Mischief said:

"You must have by your side a long *da pacem*, so that you can unbrace — carve — true men who ride by the way."

The Latin means: give peace.

Mischief meant a long dagger. Faced with a long dagger, many men will be peaceful and not fight. And if they fight, they can end up at peace six feet under the ground.

Mischief continued:

"Take their money, cut their throats, and thus overcome them.

"'I will,' say you."

"I will, sir," Mankind said.

Carrying what was left — not much — of Everyman's long coat, Nought entered the scene.

"Here is a jolly jacket!" Nought said. "What do you say?"

New Guise said:

"It is a good jacket-of-fence for a man's body."

According to the University of Michigan's online Middle English Dictionary entry for "jakke," a jakke of fence is "a short tunic worn by women."

"Hey, dog, hay! Whoop, hoo!

"Go your way lightly! You are well made for to run."

The jacket was so short that its wearer could easily defend himself by running away from danger, thus making it a jacket-of-defense.

With such a short jacket, Mankind could compete in running like a racing dog. As for providing protection against the cold, well ...

They put the short jacket on Mankind. They did not give him money from the sale of the cloth they had cut from Mankind's long coat.

Mischief said:

"Tidings! Tidings! I have spied someone coming!

"Get away from here with your stuff! We need to be gone fast! I curse the last who shall arrive to his home."

All the demons and Mankind said, "Amen!"

Mercy arrived on the scene and said, "What ho, Mankind! Flee that fellowship, I ask you!"

Mankind said:

"I shall speak with thee at another time: tomorrow morning, or the next day. We shall go forth together to keep my father's year day: the anniversary of his death."

Mankind called:

"A tapster! A tapster! Stou, stat, stou!"

According to the University of Michigan's online Middle English Dictionary, a "stou(e" is "A sacred site, religious house, monastery."

And according to the University of Michigan's online Middle English Dictionary, a "stat" is "A moral or spiritual state or condition."

Apparently, Mankind and the demons would observe the day of Mankind's father's death in an alehouse, thereby perverting the usual location and state of mind for observing the anniversary of the death of one's father.

At the arrival of Mercy, the demons had madly rushed around, causing Mischief to trip.

Mischief said:

"A mischief go with thee! Here I have a foul fall.

"Leave, get away from me, or I shall beshit you all."

New Guise shouted:

"What! How! Hostler! Hostler! Lend us a football!

"Whoop! Wow! Now! Now! Now! Now!"

A hostler takes care of horses at an inn.

The football was for USAmerican soccer.

The demons and Mankind exited.

Mankind left his prayer-beads behind, hidden by some shrubbery.

CHAPTER 3

— Scene 3 —

— Redemption —

Alone, Mercy said to himself:

"My mind is dispersed; my body trembles like the aspen leaf.

"The tears would trickle down my cheeks, were it not for your reverence."

Out of respect for you, the members of the audience, Mercy would not cry.

Mercy continued:

"The cruel visitation of death would be solace for me.

"Without rude behavior I cannot express this distress. Weeping, sighing, and sobbing would be my sustenance.

All natural nutriment — food — is to me as odious as carrion. My inward affliction renders me tedious to your presence.

"I cannot bear it calmly that Mankind is so flexible and changeable.

"Man unkind and unnatural, wherever thou be!

"For all this world could not see how to discharge thine original offence, thralldom and captivity, until God's own well-beloved Son was obedient and willing to endure every drop of His blood being shed to purge thine iniquity.

"I discommend and disallow and disapprove thine frequent mutability and changeability. To every creature thou are despised and hateful. Why are thou so uncourteous, so inconsiderate?

"Alas, and woe is me! As the weathervane that turns with the wind, so are thou convertible and changeable.

"In trust is treason; thy promise is not believable and is not credible.

"Thy perverse, corrupt ingratitude I cannot recount.

"To God and to all the holy court of Heaven, thou are despicable.

"As a noble versifier makes mention in his verse: '*Lex et natura, Christus et omnia jura / Damnant ingratum, lugent eum fore natum.*'"

The Latin means: Law and Nature, Christ and every law [justice] / Damn the ingrate, and lament that he was born.

Mercy continued:

"O good Lady and Mother of Mercy, have pity and compassion on the wretchedness of Mankind, which is so wanton and so frail! Let mercy exceed justice, dear Mother, and grant this prayer: Equity to be laid aside and mercy to prevail.

"The too sensual living that exists nowadays is reprovable, as may be made clear by the understanding of this matter.

"New Guise, Nowadays, and Nought with their alluring ways have perverted Mankind, my sweet son, I have well seen.

"Ah, if I may prevent it, Mankind shall not long remain with these cursed wretches.

"I, Mercy, his spiritual father, will proceed forth and do my natural duty.

"Our Lady, help! This manner of living is a detestable pleasure. *Vanitas vanitatum*, all is but a vanity."

The Latin means: Vanity of vanities.

Ecclesiastes 1:2 states, "*Vanity of vanities, saith the Preacher, vanity of vanities; all is vanity*" (King James Version).

Mercy continued:

"Mercy shall never be conquered by Humankind's uncourteous and ungracious way of life. With weeping tears by night and by day I will go and never cease. Won't I find him? Yes, I hope I do.

"Now God be my protection! My beloved son, where are you? Mankind, *ubi es*?"

The Latin means: where are you?

Luke 15:3-7 (King James Version) states:

3 And he spake this parable unto them, saying,

4 What man of you, having an hundred sheep, if he lose one of them, doth not leave the ninety and nine in the wilderness, and go after that which is lost, until he find it?

5 And when he hath found it, he layeth it on his shoulders, rejoicing.

6 And when he cometh home, he calleth together his friends and neighbours, saying unto them, Rejoice with me; for I have found my sheep which was lost.

7 I say unto you, that likewise joy shall be in heaven over one sinner that repenteth, more than over ninety and nine just persons, which need no repentance.

Mercy left the scene, and Mischief entered the scene.

Mischief said to Mercy's back as he left:

"My prepotent — most powerful — father, when you soupe, soupe out your messe."

According to the University of Michigan's online Middle English Dictionary, to "soupen" is "To take the evening meal, to eat supper."

And according to the University of Michigan's online Middle English Dictionary, a "messe" is "The sacrament of the Eucharist."

Mischief continued:

"You are all too-gloried in your terms — you have a considerable vocabulary of fancy words.

"You make many a lesse."

According to the University of Michigan's online Middle English Dictionary, a "les(e" is "what is false; falsehood, untruth, lying, lies."

Mischief's point may be that, to him, the mass consists of lies.

The Mass begins, *"I believe in God, the Father almighty, Creator of heaven and earth, and in Jesus Christ, his only Son, our Lord."*

All demons know that God exists.

The mass also says, *"The grace of our Lord Jesus Christ, and the love of God, and the communion of the Holy Spirit be with you all."*

The grace of God is for repentant sinners, and demons are not repentant sinners.

New Guise, Nowadays, and Nought entered the scene. They started peeing and defecating.

Mischief said to them:

"Will you hear? Mercy constantly cries, 'Mankind, *ubi es?*'

New Guise said:

"*Hic hic, hic hic, hic hic, hic hic!*"

In addition to hiccupping, New Guise was saying in Latin, "Here here!"

New Guise continued:

"That is to say: 'Here, here, here I am! Nearly dead in the creek.'"

The creek may be urine and ass-juice flowing on the ground.

New Guise continued:

"If you — Mercy — will have him, go and seek, seek, seek!"

"Don't seek overlong, for fear of losing your mind!

Nowadays said:

"If you will have Mankind, call '*domine, domine, dominus!*'"

The Latin means, O lord, O lord, the lord!

Nowadays continued:

"You must speak to the sheriff for a *cape corpus.*"

The Latin means: Seize the body.

Cape corpus is a legal warrant for an arrest.

Nowadays continued:

"Or else you must be prepared to return with *non est inventus.*"

The Latin means: He is not found.

Nowadays then said:

"What do you say, sir? My bolt is shot."

One meaning of "My bolt is shot" is "I am finished."

This is the other meaning:

Nowadays had finished talking; he had also just finished defecating. His turd was in the form of an arrow-like log. A bolt is a blunt arrow.

Nought said:

"I am doing of my needings."

He was defecating.

Nought said to Nowadays:

"Beware how you schett!"

As a verb, "schett" means 1) to aim or shoot, and 2) to shit.

According to the University of Michigan's online Middle English Dictionary, "sheten" means "To shoot (sb. oneself, an animal, a bird) with an arrow, hit; also *fig* [figurative]."

And according to the University of Michigan's online Middle English Dictionary, "sheten" also means to "cause [the bowels] to protrude from the rectum."

According to the *Oxford English Dictionary*, "shitten" means "Soiled or covered with excrement."

Nowadays had shit on Nought's foot.

Nought said:

"Fie! Fie! Fie! Damn! Damn! Damn! I have foully arrayed — covered and clothed — my foot."

Nought had just shit on his own foot.

Nought said:

"Be wise in shooting with your weapons, for God knows that my foot is foully overschett: foully shit on."

Nowadays had overshot his target and had hit Nought's foot, which was now covered over with shit — two layers.

Mischief said:

"A parliament! A parliament! Come forth. Nought, stay behind."

Mischief wanted Nowadays, New Guise, and Nought to step forward. But then he smelled what was on Nought's shoe, and so he wanted Nought to stay in the rear.

(Puns on "behind" and "rear" are intended.)

Mischief continued:

"A council — quickly!

"I am afraid Mercy will find him. How do you say, and what do you say?

"What shall we do with Mankind?"

New Guise said:

"Bah! A fly's wing! A trifle! Do you want my advice for how you can do well?

"Mankind thinks that Mercy was hanged for stealing a mare.

"Mischief, go say to him that Mercy seeks him everywhere. Mankind will hang himself, I guarantee, out of fear of a ghost."

"I assent to this plan," Mischief said. "It is wittily said and well thought-out."

Nowadays said:

"Put a noose in thy coat; soon the hanging will be done.

"Now may Saint Gabriel's mother save the patches of thy shoes. All the books in the world, if they had been opened and studied, could not have counselled us better."

Saint Gabriel is the Archangel Gabriel and the Angel of the Annunciation. He announced to Mary that she would give birth to Christ. Saint Gabriel is the patron saint of messengers. God created the angels.

Nowadays was saying that God should preserve the patches of New Guise's shoes as relics because New Guise had come up with such a good plan for getting Mankind to commit suicide.

In Dante's *Inferno*, the Suicides are punished in Circle 7, which is dedicated to punishing the Violent. The Suicides were violent against themselves.

After leaving the boiling river of blood, Dante and Virgil arrived at a gloomy wood where the Suicides were punished. The Suicides, in fact, were the grubby shrubs of the wood. They could communicate only where and when a twig or branch was broken, then they used the resulting hole as a mouth until the blood congealed.

This punishment is appropriate because by killing themselves, the Suicides gave up the privilege of self-determination. As shrubs, the Suicides have no free will because plants have no free will. This is appropriate because in life the Suicides rejected free will by committing suicide. As grubby shrubs, the Suicides cannot move around and cannot even speak unless someone breaks off a twig or branch. At the Last Judgment, the Suicides will be given back their bodies, but because they rejected their bodies when they were alive, the bodies will hang from the branches of the shrubs.

Exodus 20:13 states, "*Thou shalt not kill*" (King James Version).

Mischief exited and called, "Hey, Mankind! Come and speak with Mercy; he is here nearby."

Mischief returned quickly with Mankind.

Mankind wailed, "A rope! A rope! A rope! I am not worthy!"

Mischief said:

"Anon! Anon! Anon! Quickly! Quickly! Quickly! I have it here ready with a tree that I also have gotten ready."

The tree was a gallows-tree.

Mischief then said:

"Hold the tree, Nowadays, Nought! Take heed and be wise!"

New Guise said:

"Lo, Mankind! Do as I do; this is the new guise: the new fashion."

He demonstrated how to put the noose around the neck.

He then said:

"Adjust the rope just to thy neck; this is my advice."

A short distance away, Mercy entered the scene. He was carrying a whip.

Seeing Mercy, Mischief said, "Help thyself, Nought! Look, Mercy is here! He scares us away with a whip; we may no longer tarry."

Forgetting that he had the noose around his neck, New Guise started to run away but was stopped short by the rope.

He said:

"Crack! Crack! Crack!

"Alas, my throat! Curse you, by the Virgin Mary!

"Ah, Mercy, may Christ's greatest curse go with you, and Saint Davy!"

Saint David is the patron saint of Wales.

New Guise then said:

"Alas, my throat! You were somewhat too near to death by hanging."

The other demons returned and released New Guise from the noose, and they exited, leaving behind Mercy and Mankind.

Mercy said:

"Arise, my precious redeemed son! You are to me very dear.

"He is so frightened that it seems to me that his vital spirit is expiring."

Mankind said, "Alas, I have been so bestially disposed that I dare not appear. I am not worthy to desire to see your comforting face."

Mercy said, "Your guilty complaint wounds my heart like a lance. Dispose yourself meekly to ask for mercy, and I will assent. Yield to me neither gold nor treasure, but your humble obedience — the voluntary, willing subjection of your heart — and I am willing to give you mercy."

Mankind said:

"What! Ask for mercy yet once again?

"Alas, it would be a vile petition always to offend and always to ask for mercy. It is a childish practice. It is so abominable to rehearse my repeated transgression that I am not worthy to have mercy by any possibility."

Mankind was committing the sin of despair: He believed that his sins were so bad that God could not forgive them. But if the sinner sincerely repents, God can forgive any sin.

Mercy said:

"O Mankind, my special solace and comfort, this is a lamentable excuse.

"The dolorous, grievous tears of my heart, how they begin to mount!"

"O pierced Jesus, help thou this sinful sinner to return to grace. *Nam hec est mutacio dextre Excelsi; vertit impios et non sunt.*"

The Latin means: For this is the change of the right hand of the Most High; he overturns the impious and wicked, and they are no more.

Psalm 77:10 states, "*And I said, This is my infirmity: but I will remember the years of the right hand of the most High*" (King James Version).

Proverbs 12:7 states, "*The wicked are overthrown, and are not: but the house of the righteous shall stand*" (King James Version).

Mercy continued:

"Arise and ask for mercy, Mankind, and be a friend to me.

"Thy death shall be my heaviness; alas, it is a pity it should be thus. Thy obstinacy will exclude thee from the glorious perpetuity: from eternal life.

"Yet for my love open thy lips and say "*Miserere mei, Deus*!"

The Latin means: Have mercy on me, God!

Psalm 51 begins with "*Have mercy on me, O God*" (King James Version).

Psalms 55 and 56 each begin with "*Be merciful unto me, O God*" (King James Version).

Mankind said, "The equal, evenhanded justice of God will not permit such a sinful wretch to be revived and restored again; it would be impossible."

Mercy said:

"The justice of God will as I will, as He Himself does make clear.

"*Nolo mortem peccatoris, inquit*, if he will be reformed."

The Latin means: I do not wish the death of a sinner, he said.

Ezekiel 33:11 states, "*Say unto them, As I live, saith the Lord God, I have no pleasure in the death of the wicked; but that the wicked turn from his way and live: turn ye, turn ye from your evil ways; for why will ye die, O house of Israel?"* (King James Version).

Mankind said:

"Then give me mercy, good Mercy! What is a man without mercy? Little would be our part of Paradise if mercy did not exist.

"Good Mercy, excuse the inevitable objection of my spiritual enemy.

"The proverb says, 'The truth proves itself.'

"Alas, I have much care and concern and worry."

Mankind's spiritual enemy will object to mercy being shown to Mankind and will instead insist that Mankind has sinned and deserves to go to Hell.

Mercy said:

"God will not make you a confidant about his Last Judgment."

Mankind will have to experience the Last Judgment to learn how Mankind will be judged.

Mercy continued:

"I will not deny that Justice and Equity shall be strengthened: They will be strong in argument.

"Truth may not so cruelly proceed in his strict, exacting argument. And it is true that Mercy shall rule the matter without controversy."

At the Last Judgment, Justice and Equity will be present. Truth will present its evidence, but Mercy will make the final and decisive decision.

Mercy continued:

"Arise now and go with me in this covered walking area: this cloister.

"Incline your capacity and listen carefully; my doctrine is convenient and pertinent.

"Sin not in hope of mercy; that is a notorious crime. Don't commit a sin with the expectation that you will be forgiven.

Ecclesiastes 5:4-7 states:

4 When thou vowest a vow unto God, defer not to pay it; for he hath no pleasure in fools: pay that which thou hast vowed.

5 Better is it that thou shouldest not vow, than that thou shouldest vow and not pay.

6 Suffer not thy mouth to cause thy flesh to sin; neither say thou before the angel, that it was an error: wherefore should God be angry at thy voice, and destroy the work of thine hands?

7 For in the multitude of dreams and many words there are also divers vanities: but fear thou God.

Mercy continued:

"To trust overmuch in a prince is not appropriate."

In other words: Don't commit a sin while thinking that your value means that you deserve to be pardoned for sinning. The prince may not agree.

Psalm 146:3 states, "*Put not your trust in princes, nor in the son of man, in whom there is no help*" (King James Version).

Mercy continued:

"In hope, when you sin, you think to have mercy, beware of that venture."

In other words: Don't sin with the hope of receiving mercy: That is risky.

Mercy continued:

"The good Lord said to the lecherous woman of Canaan that the holy gospel is the authority, as we read in Scripture: *Vade et iam amplius noli peccare.*"

The Latin means: Go, and sin no more now.

John 8:10-11 (King James Version) states:

10 When Jesus had lifted up himself, and saw none but the woman, he said unto her, Woman, where are those thine accusers? hath no man condemned thee?

11 She said, No man, Lord. And Jesus said unto her, Neither do I condemn thee: go, and sin no more.

Mercy continued:

"Christ preserved this sinful woman taken in adultery. He said to her these words, 'Go, and sin no more.'

"So also to you: Go, and sin no more.

"Beware of vain confidence in mercy. Don't offend a prince because you trust in his favor, as I said before.

"If you feel yourself trapped in the snare of your spiritual enemy, ask for mercy immediately; beware of persisting in sin.

"While a wound is fresh, it proves to be curable by surgery, whereas if a wound is untreated overlong, it is the cause of great grief."

Mankind said:

"To ask for mercy and to get it: This is a precious possession.

"Shall this expeditious petition ever be allowed, as you have insight?"

In other words: Shall this speedily made request ever be granted, to your knowledge?

Mankind was not going to waste time but was going to ask for mercy quickly.

Mercy said:

"In this present life mercy is plentiful, until death makes his division of body and soul.

"But when you are gone, *usque ad minimum quadrantem* ye shall reckon your right."

The Latin means: down to the least quarter (of a small coin).

"Your right" is "what you deserve."

Matthew 5:26 states, "*Verily I say unto thee, Thou shalt by no means come out thence, till thou hast paid the uttermost farthing*" (King James Version).

Mercy continued:

"Ask for mercy and have it, while the body with the soul are joined."

Matthew 7:7 states, "*Ask, and it shall be given you; seek, and ye shall find; knock, and it shall be opened unto you:*" (King James Version).

Mercy continued:

"If you delay until your decease to ask for mercy, ye may happen to miss your desire for Paradise.

"Be repentant here on earth. Don't trust the hour of death. Think on this lesson: '*Ecce nunc tempus acceptabile, ecce nunc dies salutis.*'"

The Latin means: Now is an acceptable time. Behold, now is the day of salvation.

2 Corinthians 6:2 states, "*Now is an acceptable time. Behold, now is the day of salvation*" (King James Version).

Isaiah 49:8 states, "*Thus saith the Lord, In an acceptable time have I heard thee, and in a day of salvation have I helped thee: and I will preserve thee, and give thee for a covenant of the people, to establish the earth, to cause to inherit the desolate heritages;*" (King James Version).

Mercy continued:

"Even if you were to possess all the virtue in the world, your merits would not be deserving of the reward of the bliss above. You would not be deserving of the least joy of Heaven, not from your own effort to ascend.

"But with mercy you may ascend to Heaven. I tell you no fable; scripture proves that what I say is true."

Romans 3:23-24 (King James Version) states:

23 For all have sinned, and come short of the glory of God;

24 Being justified freely by his grace through the redemption that is in Christ Jesus.

Mankind said:

"O Mercy, my sweet solace and sole restorer, my particular beloved, you are worthy to have my love.

"For although I am undeserving and unable to plead, you are compassionate toward my inexcusable guilt.

"Ah, it grieves my heart to think how unwisely I have acted.

"Titivillus, that invisible ghost, hung his net before my eye and by his fantastic visions contrived against God's law, he caused me to obey New Guise, Nowadays, and Nought."

Mankind was placing blame on the demons, but Mankind was responsible for his actions.

Mercy said:

"Mankind, you were oblivious to my warning advice. I said to you previously that Titivillus would make an assault against you. Beware from henceforth his delusory fables.

"The proverb says, *Jacula prestita minus ledunt.*"

The Latin means: Foreseen darts wound less.

Mercy continued:

"You have three adversaries and he — Titivillus — is master of them all.

"That is to say, your adversaries are the Devil, the World, the Flesh and the Fell [Skin].

"The New Guise, Nowadays, and Nought we may call the World.

"And properly Titivillus signifies the fiend of Hell.

"The Flesh is the lecherous concupiscence of your body.

"These are your three spiritual enemies, in whom ye have put your confidence.

"They brought you to Mischief to conclude your temporal glory, as has been shown before this worshipful audience."

"Concluding your temporal glory" means "dying."

Mercy continued:

"Remember how ready I was to help you; I was not haughty, and I did not decline to help you.

"Wherefore, good son, abstain from sin forevermore after this. You may either save or damn your soul that is so precious. The choice is yours.

"*Libere velle, libere nolle.*"

The Latin means: "Freely accept, freely reject."

In other words, you have the free will to accept salvation or to reject it and instead choose damnation.

Mercy continued:

"God may not deny you the freedom to make your decision, I know.

"Beware of Titivillus and his net, and beware of all his envious will.

"Beware of your sinful pleasure that grieves your spiritual substance: your soul.

"Your body is your enemy; let him not have his will.

"Take your leave and depart when you want. May God send you good perseverance!"

Mankind said, "Since I shall depart, bless me, father, here, and then I will go. May God send us all plenty of his great mercy!"

Mercy said:

"*Dominus custodit te ab omni malo. In nomine Patris et Filii et Spritius Sancti.*

"Amen!"

The Latin means: The Lord preserves you from all evil! In the name of the Father, the Son, and the Holy Spirit."

Psalm 121:7 states, "*The Lord shall preserve thee from all evil: he shall preserve thy soul*" (King James Version).

Mankind exited.

Mercy said to you, the audience:

"Worshipful sovereigns, I have done my special duty.

"Mankind has been delivered from evil by my benevolent protection.

"May God preserve him from all wicked captivity and send him grace to extinguish his sensual disposition.

"Now for love of Him Who for us received His humanity and took human form, search your ways of life with due and thorough examination.

"Think and remember that the world is but a vanity, as is proved daily by diverse changes.

"Mankind is wretched; he has sufficient proof of that. Therefore, may God grant all of you *per suam misericordiam* — through His mercy — that you may be companions with the angels above and so that you may have for your portion *vitam eternam* — eternal life.

"Amen!"

NOTES
— Scene 1 —

MISCHIEF

My dame seyde my name was Raffe;

(line 51)

Source of Above:

Bevington, David. *Medieval Drama*. Atlanta, etc.: Houghton Mifflin Company. 1975. Includes *Mankind*. P. 905.

"Dame" means "mother," and God created the angels, some of whom rebelled against Him and became demons, such as Mischief.

Is God a mother?

According to Ian Ramsey, we can talk about God in terms of models. A model is a way of speaking about God that allows us to speak positively about Him. For example, if I call God "Father," I am using "Father" as a model. I am saying that in some sense God is like a male parent. The use of "Father" as a model gives me a way of speaking and thinking about God.

The first type of model is related to the family; for example, God is described in terms of these models:

Father
Mother
Husband
Friend

Why use family models? Why use these models that are associated with home and friends? As an example, let us take the model of Father. What can we learn from the description of God as our Father? When you have a loving Father (and God is described as loving us), you have a Father who takes pains over you. Often this means that your father gives you rules to follow and punishes you if you don't obey the rules. Chances are, everyone reading this has been grounded at one time or another. Similarly, God — Our Father Which Art in Heaven — has given us rules to follow. (Of course, when God grounds you because you broke His rules, it's for eternity!) When things are going well for us, as they often do, it's as if we had a loving Father watching out for us.

As another example, let's take a true friend. (God, of course, is true.) Characteristics of a true friend include reliability and trustworthiness. In some aspects, the universe is like that. For example, take seed-time and harvest. One thing that we can always be sure of in Athens, Ohio, is that Winter will be succeeded by Spring. Winter may seem as if it will never end, but eventually it does end and is succeeded by Spring.

In these models of home and friends, Ramsey writes that "the human case acts as a catalyst for the cosmic case, to generate a cosmic disclosure." The term "cosmic disclosure" is important in Ramsey's thought. We can look around us, and often we can learn something about the transcendent reality that lies behind the physical reality that we experience with our senses.

Ramsey goes on to discuss two more types of model:

The second type of model is related to work and crafts, and professions; for example, God is described in terms of these models:

Shepherd
Farmer
Dairymaid
Fuller (Laundress)
Builder
Potter
Fisherman
Tradesman
Physician

Teacher and Scribe
Nurse
Metal Worker

The third type of model is related to the Nation; for example, God is described in terms of these models:

King
Warrior
Judge

For Further Information: Ian Ramsey, *Christian Empiricism.* Grand Rapids, Mich.: William B. Eerdsman Publishing Company, 1974.

— Scene 1 —

NEW GUISE

Ye fede yowr hors in mesure; ye are a wise man!
I trow, and ye were the kingys palfrey-man
A good horse shulde be gesunne.
(lines 250-252)
Source of Above:

Bevington, David. *Medieval Drama.* Atlanta, etc.: Houghton Mifflin Company. 1975. Includes *Mankind.* P. 912.

Spelling was not standardized in the Middle Ages. If *gesunne* means *geason,* then it means "scarce." In that case, New Guise is saying that Mercy's moderation in feeding the horses would result in few good horses.

But if *gesunne* means *gesumme,* from Old Norse *gørsemi,* then it means "plentiful." In that case, New Guise is saying that Mercy's moderation in feeding the horses would result in many good horses.

The Old Norse *gørsimi* means "treasure."

F.J. Furnivall and Alfred W. Pollard, in their *The Macro Plays,* made this footnote on "gesumme":

gersuma, 'gressoms,' *O.N.* gørsemi, *plentiful.*

Given that demons are more likely to criticize a priest than to praise one, *gesunne* may mean *geason:* scarce. In addition, New Guise's use of the word "wise" to describe Mercy would be ironic.

On the other hand, New Guise has admitted to overfeeding his wife with bad results, and Mercy does not overfeed horses, so *gesunne* may mean *gesumme:* plentiful.

In real life, of course, overfeeding horses is very bad. Overfeeding horses can cause colic, which can be fatal.

Kathleen M. Ashley and Gerard NeCastro write in a note on *A good horse shulde be gesunne* (line 252):

New Guise, disagreeing with Mercy, claims, on practical grounds, that a good horse should be well fed. If Mercy kept the king's horses, he suggests, the king would have few horses. "Gesunne" is one of the most difficult words in the play. L's choice of *geason* means "scarce"; Furnivall and Pollard's choice of *gesumme* derives from the Old Norse *gørsemi*, which means plentiful (*Macro Plays*, p. 10). But L's reading as "scarce" makes the best sense.

L is G.A. Lester, *Mankind* in *Three Late Medieval Morality Plays*.

David Bruce believes that Mercy advocates moderation in a horse's diet. Such a diet would keep the horse well-fed, but not overfed. It is possible that New Guise is deliberately misunderstanding Mercy as saying that horses should be starved.

For More Information:

Mankind. Edited by Kathleen M. Ashley and Gerard NeCastro. Kalamazoo, MI: Medieval Institute Publications, 2010. P. 50.

Furnivall, F.J., and Alfred W. Pollard, eds. *The Macro Plays*, EETS e.s.91. London: Oxford University Press, 1904. P. 10.

Lester, G.A., ed. *Three Late Medieval Morality Plays*. London: A & C Black, 1997. Print.

Lester, G.A. ed. *Mankind*. London: Bloomsbury, 2013. Web. Subscription required.

https://www-dramaonlinelibrary-com.proxy.library.ohio.edu/playtext-overview?docid=do-9781408169223&tocid=do-9781408169223-div-00000021

***

Can *gesumme* be a portmanteau word? David Bruce doesn't think so, but see the following:

According to the *Oxford English Dictionary*, "gest" means:

> *plural.* Notable deeds or actions, exploits (later also *singular*, a deed, exploit); esp. the deeds *of* a person or people as narrated or recorded, history. *Obsolete* exc. *archaic.*

> Action, performance.

> Bearing, carriage, mien.

According to the *Oxford English Dictionary*, "summe" means:

> A quantity, number, total.

> A quantity of goods, livestock, etc., having an agreed or recognized value; a defined or standardized unit of a particular commodity.

According to the *Oxford English Dictionary*, "sum" [Middle English "summe"] means:

> A unit of weight used to measure the quantity of certain commodities, esp. crops.

According to the *Oxford English Dictionary*, "sin" [Middle English "sunne"] means:

> An act which is regarded as a transgression of the divine law and an offence against God; a violation (esp. wilful or deliberate) of some religious or moral principle.

If "gest" could be used as an adjective (a usage not in the *Oxford English Dictionary*), could "gesumme" mean "a notable weight"? If so, we would have to wonder what a "notable weight" would be. If New Guise is accusing Mercy of starving horses, then the horses would have an unhealthy low weight.

According to the *Oxford English Dictionary*, "sun" [Old Friscian "sunne"] means:

> In figurative contexts and extended metaphors in which the shining of the sun represents or symbolizes glory, joy, good fortune, etc.

The first quotation for this meaning from is 1579, but if "gesumme" uses that meaning, and if New Guise is unironically using "wise" to describe Mercy, then he is saying that Mercy's feeding of horses would be a notable act that results in good horses that are notable "suns": They would be notably good horses.

— Scene 2 —

The Saint Francis coat anecdote comes from this source:

John Deedy, *A Book of Catholic Anecdotes*. Allen, Texas: Thomas More, 1997. P. 86.

This anecdote and the other anecdotes about coats are told in David Bruce's own words.

Selling a Painting

Edwin Forrest, a famous 19th-century actor, did many good deeds. One winter, he found an ill, impoverished man shivering in the cold. Mr. Forrest wrapped him in his overcoat and got help for him. On another occasion, a poor woman tried to sell him a painting. Mr. Forrest suspected that it was the only thing of value she had, so he took the woman and her family, put them in a comfortable apartment — at his expense — and hung the painting on one of the apartment's walls.

Source: Wagenknecht, Edward. *Merely Players*. Norman, OK: University of Oklahoma Press, 1966. P. 118.

"Dear Santa, I'm an Orphan"

When Eddie Cantor was eight, he wrote in answer to a newspaper contest awarding Christmas presents to whoever wrote the best letter. Eddie wrote, "Dear Santa, I'm an orphan. I have no mother or father. I live with my grandmother who is very poor. I have no warm clothes. I would like a pair of rubber boots, an overcoat, and a sled. That is all I want for Christmas." Christmas came, and that was all. Eddie sat on his front stoop, hating everything, especially the newspaper that sponsored the contest. Finally, at the end of the day, a *New York Journal* truck drove up and Eddie got his Christmas presents and became a fan of William Randolph Hearst. As an adult, Mr. Cantor became a famous comedian and entertainer and an eager participant in raising money for charity. In his book *This Way, Miss* George Jessel tells a story that illustrates his friend Eddie Cantor's prowess at raising money for charity: "Once upon a time, in a little village, there was a group in the market place, talking of strong men. One, to show his prowess, took an orange, squeezed it to nothingness in one movement, and got a glass of orange juice. Then Cantor took what was left of the orange, and he squeezed it, got two quarts of orange juice and sixty dollars in cash."

Sources:

Cantor, Eddie. *Take My Life*. Written with Jane Kesner Ardmore. Garden City, NY: Doubleday, 1957. Pp. 14-15.

Jessel, George. *This Way, Miss*. New York: Henry Holt and Company, 1955. P. 89.

Enrico Caruso's Kindness

Tenor Enrico Caruso was capable of great kindness. He once saw a beggar shivering outside his hotel, so he gave him his fur-lined coat. Mr. Caruso owned many clothes, so many that people asked why he had such a large wardrobe. To such inquiries, he replied, "Two reasons. First reason, I like. Second reason, other people like. Also, I give to people who ask."

Source: Matheopoulos, Helena. *The Great Tenors From Caruso to the Present*. New York: St. Martin's Press, 1999. Pp. 15-16.

APPENDIX A: FAIR USE

§ 107. Limitations on exclusive rights: Fair use
Release date: 2004-04-30
Notwithstanding the provisions of sections 106 and 106A, the fair use of a copyrighted work, including such use by reproduction in copies or phonorecords or by any other means specified by that section, for purposes such as criticism, comment, news reporting, teaching (including multiple copies for classroom use), scholarship, or research, is not an infringement of copyright. In determining whether the use made of a work in any particular case is a fair use the factors to be considered shall include —

(1) the purpose and character of the use, including whether such use is of a commercial nature or is for nonprofit educational purposes;

(2) the nature of the copyrighted work;

(3) the amount and substantiality of the portion used in relation to the copyrighted work as a whole; and

(4) the effect of the use upon the potential market for or value of the copyrighted work.

The fact that a work is unpublished shall not itself bar a finding of fair use if such finding is made upon consideration of all the above factors.

Source of Fair Use information:
http://www.law.cornell.edu/uscode/17/107.html

APPENDIX B: ABOUT THE AUTHOR

It was a dark and stormy night. Suddenly a cry rang out, and on a hot summer night in 1954, Josephine, wife of Carl Bruce, gave birth to a boy — me. Unfortunately, this young married couple allowed Reuben Saturday, Josephine's brother, to name their first-born. Reuben, aka "The Joker," decided that Bruce was a nice name, so he decided to name me Bruce Bruce. I have gone by my middle name — David — ever since.

Being named Bruce David Bruce hasn't been all bad. Bank tellers remember me very quickly, so I don't often have to show an ID. It can be fun in charades, also. When I was a counselor as a teenager at Camp Echoing Hills in Warsaw, Ohio, a fellow counselor gave the signs for "sounds like" and "two words," then she pointed to a bruise on her leg twice. Bruise Bruise? Oh yeah, Bruce Bruce is the answer!

Uncle Reuben, by the way, gave me a haircut when I was in kindergarten. He cut my hair short and shaved a small bald spot on the back of my head. My mother wouldn't let me go to school until the bald spot grew out again.

Of all my brothers and sisters (six in all), I am the only transplant to Athens, Ohio. I was born in Newark, Ohio, and have lived all around Southeastern Ohio. However, I moved to Athens to go to Ohio University and have never left.

At Ohio U, I never could make up my mind whether to major in English or Philosophy, so I got a bachelor's degree with a double major in both areas, then I added a Master of Arts degree in English and a Master of Arts degree in Philosophy. Yes, I have my MAMA degree.

Currently, and for a long time to come (I eat fruits and veggies), I am spending my retirement writing books such as *Nadia Comaneci: Perfect 10*, *The Funniest People in Comedy*, *Homer's* Iliad: *A Retelling in Prose*, and *William Shakespeare's* Hamlet: *A Retelling in Prose*.

If all goes well, I will publish one or two books a year for the rest of my life. (On the other hand, a good way to make God laugh is to tell Her your plans.)

By the way, my sister Brenda Kennedy writes romances such as *A New Beginning* and *Shattered Dreams*.

APPENDIX C: SOME BOOKS BY DAVID BRUCE

Retellings of a Classic Work of Literature

Arden of Faversham: *A Retelling*

Ben Jonson's The Alchemist: *A Retelling*

Ben Jonson's The Arraignment, or Poetaster: *A Retelling*

Ben Jonson's Bartholomew Fair: *A Retelling*

Ben Jonson's The Case is Altered: *A Retelling*

Ben Jonson's Catiline's Conspiracy: *A Retelling*

Ben Jonson's The Devil is an Ass: *A Retelling*

Ben Jonson's Epicene: *A Retelling*

Ben Jonson's Every Man in His Humor: *A Retelling*

Ben Jonson's Every Man Out of His Humor: *A Retelling*

Ben Jonson's The Fountain of Self-Love, or Cynthia's Revels: *A Retelling*

Ben Jonson's The Magnetic Lady, or Humors Reconciled: *A Retelling*

Ben Jonson's The New Inn, or The Light Heart: *A Retelling*

Ben Jonson's Sejanus' Fall: *A Retelling*

Ben Jonson's The Staple of News: *A Retelling*

Ben Jonson's A Tale of a Tub: *A Retelling*

Ben Jonson's Volpone, or the Fox: *A Retelling*

Christopher Marlowe's Complete Plays: Retellings

Christopher Marlowe's Dido, Queen of Carthage: *A Retelling*

Christopher Marlowe's Doctor Faustus: *Retellings of the 1604 A-Text and of the 1616 B-Text*

Christopher Marlowe's Edward II: *A Retelling*

Christopher Marlowe's The Massacre at Paris: *A Retelling*

Christopher Marlowe's The Rich Jew of Malta: *A Retelling*

Christopher Marlowe's Tamburlaine, Parts 1 and 2: *Retellings*

Dante's Divine Comedy: *A Retelling in Prose*

Dante's Inferno: *A Retelling in Prose*

Dante's Purgatory: *A Retelling in Prose*

Dante's Paradise: *A Retelling in Prose*

The Famous Victories of Henry V: *A Retelling*

From the Iliad *to the* Odyssey: *A Retelling in Prose of Quintus of Smyrna's* Posthomerica

George Chapman, Ben Jonson, and John Marston's Eastward Ho! *A Retelling*

Thomas Middleton and Thomas Dekker's The Roaring Girl: *A Retelling*
Thomas Middleton and William Rowley's The Changeling: *A Retelling*
The Trojan War and Its Aftermath: Four Ancient Epic Poems
Virgil's Aeneid: *A Retelling in Prose*
William Shakespeare's 5 Late Romances: Retellings in Prose
William Shakespeare's 10 Histories: Retellings in Prose
William Shakespeare's 11 Tragedies: Retellings in Prose
William Shakespeare's 12 Comedies: Retellings in Prose
William Shakespeare's 38 Plays: Retellings in Prose
William Shakespeare's 1 Henry IV, aka Henry IV, Part 1: *A Retelling in Prose*
William Shakespeare's 2 Henry IV, aka Henry IV, Part 2: *A Retelling in Prose*
William Shakespeare's 1 Henry VI, aka Henry VI, Part 1: *A Retelling in Prose*
William Shakespeare's 2 Henry VI, aka Henry VI, Part 2: *A Retelling in Prose*
William Shakespeare's 3 Henry VI, aka Henry VI, Part 3: *A Retelling in Prose*
William Shakespeare's All's Well that Ends Well: *A Retelling in Prose*
William Shakespeare's Antony and Cleopatra: *A Retelling in Prose*
William Shakespeare's As You Like It: *A Retelling in Prose*
William Shakespeare's The Comedy of Errors: *A Retelling in Prose*
William Shakespeare's Coriolanus: *A Retelling in Prose*
William Shakespeare's Cymbeline: *A Retelling in Prose*
William Shakespeare's Hamlet: *A Retelling in Prose*
William Shakespeare's Henry V: *A Retelling in Prose*
William Shakespeare's Henry VIII: *A Retelling in Prose*
William Shakespeare's Julius Caesar: *A Retelling in Prose*
William Shakespeare's King John: *A Retelling in Prose*
William Shakespeare's King Lear: *A Retelling in Prose*
William Shakespeare's Love's Labor's Lost: *A Retelling in Prose*
William Shakespeare's Macbeth: *A Retelling in Prose*
William Shakespeare's Measure for Measure: *A Retelling in Prose*
William Shakespeare's The Merchant of Venice: *A Retelling in Prose*
William Shakespeare's The Merry Wives of Windsor: *A Retelling in Prose*
William Shakespeare's A Midsummer Night's Dream: *A Retelling in Prose*
William Shakespeare's Much Ado About Nothing: *A Retelling in Prose*
William Shakespeare's Othello: *A Retelling in Prose*
William Shakespeare's Pericles, Prince of Tyre: *A Retelling in Prose*
William Shakespeare's Richard II: *A Retelling in Prose*
William Shakespeare's Richard III: *A Retelling in Prose*
William Shakespeare's Romeo and Juliet: *A Retelling in Prose*
William Shakespeare's The Taming of the Shrew: *A Retelling in Prose*

William Shakespeare's The Tempest: *A Retelling in Prose*
William Shakespeare's Timon of Athens: *A Retelling in Prose*
William Shakespeare's Titus Andronicus: *A Retelling in Prose*
William Shakespeare's Troilus and Cressida: *A Retelling in Prose*
William Shakespeare's Twelfth Night: *A Retelling in Prose*
William Shakespeare's The Two Gentlemen of Verona: *A Retelling in Prose*
William Shakespeare's The Two Noble Kinsmen: *A Retelling in Prose*
William Shakespeare's The Winter's Tale: *A Retelling in Prose*